SADDLE WISE

1

RAINY DAY RESCUE

Inda
Schaenen

RP|KIDS
PHILADELPHIA · LONDON

Dedication

This story is for horses big and small,
both real and imagined.

Library of Congress Control Number: 2008933253

ISBN 978-0-7624-3351-3

Cover illustration by Robert Papp
Cover and interior design by Frances J. Soo Ping Chow
Icons illustrated by Rich Kelly
Edited by Kelli Chipponeri
Typography: Affair and Berthold Baskerville

Published by Running Press Kids,
an imprint of Running Press Book Publishers
2300 Chestnut Street
Philadelphia, PA 19103-4371

Visit us on the web!
www.runningpress.com

chapter

Aunt Patti's knuckles were white against the steering wheel as she leaned forward to see through the foggy patch of windshield. Her mouth was turned down in a frown of concentration. Behind fashionably heavy-rimmed glasses, her nearsighted eyes squinted to get a better look. It had been raining for weeks—all spring, it seemed—and now the water was coming down in sheets.

"I swear, April," she said, "if we make it into St. Louis in one piece, it'll be a miracle. Push that defogger button for me, will you, please?"

A big white Suburban passed us, splashing our car with oily gray highway water. I had never seen conditions on Interstate 54 this dangerous or my normally bubbly aunt this tense. We were heading into town to spend Saturday at my grandma's house. Today was May 1, her sixtieth birthday, and all my relatives were coming to celebrate. Our car smelled like brownies—Aunt Patti had pulled a triple batch out of the oven right before we left home. The pans were still cooling at the bottom of an old UPS box in the backseat. Even when I closed my eyes and tried to concentrate on the warm, sweet smell of chocolate, I could hear the windshield wipers swinging back and forth at top speed, drumming up the tension. Even when she stopped talking altogether, Aunt Patti's nervousness was contagious. I opened my eyes and peered out the windshield.

"Thank goodness," Aunt Patti said, pushing her glasses up her nose with one hand. "Finally people are slowing down. I don't know why in the world people think they can drive sixty and seventy miles an hour in rain like this, it's just craz—oh!"

From somewhere in the distance ahead I heard a skid, then an awful crashing, crunching sound. Aunt Patti slammed on the brakes and swung her right arm across my chest. At the same moment I was pressed tight against my seat belt, which had locked across my torso. For an instant I wondered whether we were going to smash into the car in front of us. Certain that an accident was inevitable, I squeezed my eyes closed and held my breath.

We screeched to a halt, and for a few moments there was a strange silence. Then the shouting began.

I looked at Aunt Patti. Her face, usually so bright and smiley, was twisted and pale. When she turned to stare back at me, she seemed on the verge of tears.

"What's going on?" I asked.

"Not sure, hon," she replied, her voice shaky.

The people in the car ahead of us jumped out and ran to see what had happened. "Grab your poncho, April. I think we need to see what's what."

Aunt Patti turned off our car engine and locked the doors behind us. The next few moments were surreal: I knew something terrible had happened, but didn't know what. I felt a mixture of curiosity and dread, like when you're watching a character in a movie approach a crime scene. Aunt Patti and I were okay, but I knew that someone else wasn't. Part of me definitely did not want to see what lay ahead; another part did. That was the only reason I managed to put one foot in front of the other.

Several cars farther up, we saw something you only see in black-and-white pictures in newspapers. A big tractor-trailer was lying on its side, half in the eastbound direction of Interstate 54 and half crashed through the barrier on the westbound side of the highway. Around the broken and dented trailer, small rivers of blood were forming wide pools. Huge dark shapes lay in the blood, screened by the ceaseless rain. At first I thought the shapes were sofas or chairs, but then some of the shapes started to move. I felt my arm pulled in another direction and heard Aunt Patti cry out.

"Oh, good Lord, April, these poor people got thrown from their cars, too. I'm going to see how I can help. You go back to our car." She jammed the keys in my hand and floated off in her purple poncho, a blur in the rain.

The accident scene was confusing and hard to make out. If I hadn't overheard a stranger nearby, I doubt I could have made sense of what I was looking at.

"Horses," the voice said. "That trailer was haulin' horses. Looks like forty or fifty of 'em. Must be a dozen or so killed. Hard to tell."

Another voice replied, "Driver's dead. And a few others in these here cars are pretty beat up. Here come the paramedics."

Lights flashed through the fog and the rain, and I heard sirens screaming. I was supposed to go back to the car, but I felt myself being pulled forward with the same gnawing and relentless dread, like when I completely forget to study for a test but have to march into class and take it anyway. There was no way I was going to turn around. Ever since my birthday the September before, Aunt Patti had been accusing me of "turning teen" on her. I knew she was usually joking, but there was something real about the way she said it. Thirteen did feel different from twelve. I did not want to stand there and be told what had happened after the fact. I had to see for myself.

Everyone was so busy paying attention to the injured people that no one noticed me approach where the horses were lying. It looked like the pictures of a Civil War battlefield that we discussed in sixth grade social studies. At least twelve horses had been thrown from the trailer and were scattered in bizarre positions on the ground. Legs kicked in the air as a few tried to get back upright. Others lay still on their backs, already dead. Many more were still sandwiched in the overturned trailer. A few were buried under others or pinned under the debris of the crashed truck. I heard a few of the horses panting and blowing as they kicked at the sides of the trailer. The sharp, thunderous crack made me shiver.

Even though I lived in Plattsburgh, where everyone either owned a horse, rode a horse, or stabled horses, I was no horse girl. Actually, down to my very core, I was totally afraid of them. Aunt Patti had tried to help me overcome my fear, but it was no use.

"It was like you just got stamped in the heart by what happened to your parents and wouldn't let yourself get over it," she would say. "Which is a shame, really, because Mary Beth and Harry loved those animals. I know they'd wish for you to follow in their footsteps, but it's just not meant to be, I guess."

What happened back when I was four years old was a freak accident, and I only heard the story in depth when I was old enough to understand. It was a hot August day, and my dad and mom were preparing for a training session with a new bay filly that was being boarded at the stable they managed. My mom was already in the saddle when she asked my dad to shorten her left stirrup, like she had countless times before. At the same time, the filly accidentally stepped forward into a nest of yellow jackets. The hive swarmed up and started stinging the filly and my mom. The filly spooked and reared, twirling like a tornado. My mom was jolted from the saddle onto the ground, and her neck snapped upon landing. Meanwhile, the filly's legs got tangled with my dad's, who had been trying to pull my mom clear of the hooves. When the filly landed back down on all four legs, one hoof crushed my dad's thigh right over his femoral artery. I was in fifth grade before I understood why this detail was so important—blood pumps so quickly through this artery that it was impossible to stop the bleeding. By the time the emergency helicopter arrived, both my parents were dead. My dad's youngest sister, Aunt Patti, moved out to Plattsburgh from St. Louis to take care of me and we've lived together ever since.

Since then I had known a couple of kids whose mothers

died of cancer. I knew one boy in the grade below mine whose father was killed in a car accident. There were kids at my school whose parents drank too much, hit them, or lost their jobs. Obviously, I was not the only person to have to deal with bad luck or messed-up parents. Some of those kids turned sullen and asocial. They kind of shut down. Some of them became teachers' pets, as if to prove that they could get *some* adult to like them, if not their own parents. One boy whose mom died was insanely good at football, the hero of our middle-school team. This other girl whose mom ran off and left her with a creepy stepfather was totally disruptive in class and mean to just about everybody. There were a thousand and one ways kids could suffer, but I don't think what had happened to my parents made me any different at school or with my friends. Basically, all it did was make me hate and fear horses. That was it. As far as I was concerned, a horse had killed my parents and I wanted nothing to do with them. Ever. Which in Plattsburgh, Missouri, made me a misfit.

Yet for some reason, standing in the rain in my yellow poncho, looking at all those poor, suffering creatures strewn along the highway, my hatred and fear started to wash away, leaving me confused and disoriented. People, sounds, and images swirled around me as if my eyes and ears couldn't get their signals straight.

Rain dripped from the rim of my poncho hood and I raised my hand to wipe my eyes. Just then something nudged the back of my shoulder and pushed me off balance. An emergency worker shoving me out of the way? I caught myself, sidestepped, turned around, and found before me the long muzzle of a horse. The animal's nostrils were covered in blood, and one eye was bruised and swollen shut. I could just make out the horse's chestnut coat and a big, diamond-shaped white patch on its forehead. I was face-to-face with the very thing I had always feared. I looked into its open eye and saw a deep brown pool of pain.

I froze.

The horse had lowered its muzzle to get my attention, but now, with its head held high, the animal was much taller than me. It stamped one heavy, mud-caked hoof, and my stomach swooped. I stood petrified. Even if I had been able to scream, nobody would have heard me. Too much was going on all around us. That painful eye stared at me, and the longer I looked, the more I saw. A pinkish mixture of blood and rainwater dripped down the white patch, staining the horse's forehead. It seemed to be coming from a deep gash by its ear. I wanted to back away, but sensed that I needed to stay. A second later, the horse swished his tail and rainwater splashed my hood, snapping me out of my daze. I reached out with the back of my shaking fingers and stroked the velvety spot between his bleeding nostrils. I had never felt anything so soft in my entire life.

chapter

2

That moment in time seemed to stretch and slow like an underwater dream. I couldn't lift my hand from the warm, wet nose. The horse turned his head to stare at me with his other mesmerizing eye, as if he was sizing me up.

"Hey!" a voice called. "You!"

Startled, I turned toward the crush of people, horses, and wreckage. A guy in a backward baseball cap and a blue nylon jacket was gesturing in my direction.

"Yeah, you. Lead that guy over there. We're trying to pull the survivors together and get them off the road."

I turned back to the horse with the bloody face.

"Yeah," the guy in the baseball cap hollered impatiently. "That guy. Right in front of you."

The horse lowered his head to my shoulder again, sending chills of fear down to my toes. I forced myself to reach up and stroke his neck. I was on the side of his closed eye but saw his ears pricked and listening. How was I supposed to get this huge animal to move anywhere at all?

"We're supposed to move," I said aloud, as if the horse

could understand me. "Would you maybe consider following me over there?"

I could not believe what I was saying. Who did I think I was talking to? There was nothing to grip for leading him—no rope around his neck or halter around his face. I put my hand gingerly on his mane and gripped a matted hank of hair. Luckily, when I took the first step, the horse turned to follow me. We walked side by side—me gently pulling on his wet mane and the horse carefully following my lead.

Traffic had come to a complete halt now that both sides of the highway were shut down. Police cars and fire trucks were pulled over on the gravel shoulder with their lights flashing. Many of the horses were starting to make unnatural screechy sounds. The man in the baseball cap bossed everyone around, ordering people to coax the animals to the grass on the eastbound side. We made a dismal parade—some of the horses were limping, their heads lowered. Others were rolling their eyes nervously, straining against the movements of the volunteers. As we walked, I saw a black-and-white horse stumble over a piece of metal before regaining its balance. To my surprise, I noticed that the person escorting that horse was Aunt Patti.

As we moved closer to the gathering on the roadside, I

felt fear surging inside me again. What if they all began to rear or stampede? What if the horse I was leading yanked his head away from my hand and trampled my foot? Aunt Patti was too far away to help, and I had no idea how much control I actually had over the horse at my side. Fighting back tears, I clutched a little more of the mane in my hand.

"That's it. Over here," a tall woman was saying to all the people walking with horses. She was waving her arms like the workers who guide airplanes into their proper slot at the airport. Aunt Patti brought the pinto into line.

"That's it. Good job," the woman said encouragingly.

Aunt Patti nodded and turned around. When she saw me, her eyes popped—me guiding an injured horse was probably the last thing she expected to see. I couldn't exactly smile back at her—I was concentrating on what I was doing—but I did somehow flap my free hand in a weak wave to show her I was more or less okay.

The steady rain made it impossible to see clearly. To get in the position the lady wanted, I put one hand on the horse's neck and leaned into his shoulder, hoping he would follow all the others. I stared down at my muddy tennis shoes to make sure they didn't get stepped on. Amazingly, as if he knew what I was trying to get him to do, the horse lined himself up beside the horse on the end. Then he shook his head, and all down the row the other horses shook their heads. Mimicking what I saw the other people doing, I faced him. This was how we remained, two lines facing each other, one of people and one of horses. We comforted our horses, speaking softly and stroking their bowed heads. The man next to me turned to the man next to him.

"Humane Society people are on the way."

"I heard that, too. Seems these guys were on their way to Illinois."

"Illinois?"

"There's a horse meat processor there. A Belgian outfit. Only three in the country. Two in Texas and one in Illinois, if you can believe it. They slaughter and process 'em and export the meat for consumption."

"You gotta be kidding."

"That's what I heard. The horses that didn't make it today would have been gone in a week anyway."

I swallowed and looked at the bloody face in front of me. His bangs were all matted together with dirt and blood, but he was alive and breathing. His unblinking eye stared straight into mine. Could it really be that a brush with death had saved this animal and all the others from being slaughtered? One second they were on their way to a meatpacking plant and the next second—thanks to a horrible accident they had barely survived—they had a second chance at life.

For some reason, this made me think of Lowell. Complicated ideas always made me think of Lowell.

Lowell Cheever lived next door, and we had been friends for as long as I could remember. When we were little, we would play for hours in his backyard. He had one of those cheap hand-me-down sets from the sixties, the kind made up of poles that were all rusty and wobbly at the joints. There was a swing, a dented slide, and a double swing, the kind where two people sit facing each other and pump back and forth. Lowell and I would pretend that we were runaways who lived in a tree house (the top of the slide) and pickpocketed money from rich people before hurrying away in our getaway car (the double swing). Sometimes we would take trips to other places and escape from wild animals or dragons (climbing the poles) whose features grew incredibly unrealistic over the years as we read more and more fantasy books. My dog, Chase, a spaniel-retriever mix, played the role of wild beast or tame partner in crime. Sometimes he played the long-lost baby brother we rescued from an evil foster mother. Chase was a pretty decent actor.

Lowell and I spent a lot of time in his backyard or at my house. In those days both his parents worked. His mom and dad were at the Chrysler plant in Fenton, where they had met on the assembly line making minivans. After Lowell was born, they took different shifts so someone could always be home with him. But by the time we were five, they were both forced to work late-night shifts, four P.M. to midnight or midnight to eight A.M. Aunt Patti and Lowell's parents worked it out so that they would pay her to watch Lowell when we weren't in school. As we got older and he could technically stay home alone, Aunt Patti refused to take money from them, but still insisted he stay with us as much as possible.

"I'm home anyway for April," she'd say. "And it does me a favor to have a friend for her to play with."

Aunt Patti owned a flower shop—Room for Blooms— where she worked during the hours we were in school. At home, while Lowell and I played, Aunt Patti worked in her garden. In the winter, when the ground was frozen and our yard was a mess of brown sticks, shriveled groundcover, and pruned bushes, Aunt Patti spent time on her other hobby, which was making scrapbooks. She would pick a subject that interested her, like honey, and pull together pictures and descriptions from magazines, the Internet, and brochures to make a scrapbook that would tell the whole story about honey. The honey book was filled with facts about bees and their life in the hive, the flowers that bees pollinated, the various flavors of honey, the ways honey has been used throughout history, and the incredible things the queen bee can do. She also included examples of honey-related folklore. If Lowell and I ever got bored in the afternoon, we would hang out with Aunt Patti and she would let us snip pictures and rubber cement them onto the heavy pages of her most current scrapbook. I loved watching her strong fingers at work. Working with soil and plants all day made them that way, she said. "Your dad had these hands, too," she said. "But his hand strength came from working horses, and I was only happy digging in dirt." When Aunt Patti told me things like this, I would wonder if family traits like strong hands would somehow find their way to me.

Lowell was the only person I could talk to about my parents. Aunt Patti would get misty and closemouthed. The St. Louis family always seemed to feel sorry for me, which made me feel worse. From time to time I complained about how frustrating it was not to have enough memories of my mom and dad. When I was younger, I sometimes wondered if they had really existed. However I felt, I could always count on Lowell to listen.

Things changed when we got to sixth grade. Around that time money became a problem for Lowell's parents. First his father lost his job, and then his mother's hours got cut back. Plattsburgh was not exactly a thriving metropolis and jobs were scarce, especially after the big manufacturers started closing down and moving out of the country. Lowell's mother—I call her Miz Fran—got a job with a cleaning service in St. Louis, which I knew didn't pay well and meant she was gone a lot. Meanwhile, Lowell was starting to withdraw into himself. At school he seemed constantly angry. He no longer wanted to hang out with me at home, or be seen hanging out with me at school. He had always been kind of small and soft for a boy, with thick blondish hair that older ladies made a fuss over, but overnight he seemed to grow in all directions at once. Now he moved more slowly, in a heavy and awkward way. His hands and feet were huge, and even though he wore baggy shirts you could tell his abs were no six-pack.

Sometimes, through my bedroom window, I heard Lowell's dad yelling at him and his mom. I never heard Miz Fran yell back, but I did hear Lowell. I was worried, and I could tell Aunt Patti was, too. After winter break Lowell started arriving late for school. He looked tired, as if he hadn't slept. I knew enough about his habits to know

19

that it was probably the computer keeping him up, but whether he was playing games or surfing the Internet, I had no idea.

The Monday before the highway accident, we had been talking in Social Studies about the Bill of Rights. Mr. Millstadt, our teacher, asked how we thought our lives would be different without these rights. Lowell didn't raise his hand before blurting something about rights depending on who you were. Mr. Millstadt scolded him for his attitude but Lowell just lowered his head and muttered, "What's the point?"

When I heard the man say the horses had been bound for a slaughterhouse, I imagined Lowell's bitter voice saying, "What's the point?" Here we stood in the pouring rain for the sake of animals that were destined to die anyway. What was the point of having survived an awful accident only to be turned into horse meat?

The rain had dripped inside my poncho and I kept shivering. I peered down the line and tried to catch Aunt Patti's eye, but she was paying attention to the pinto's right front leg, which he held off the ground as if something was wrong with his knee. I looked at the horse in front of me and put one hand on his nose and the other under his chin. I patted the side of his neck, amazed at how firm, strong, and warm the wet hair felt under my hand. While doing this, I studied his legs. They appeared to be fine, but what did I know? The horse nodded his head up and down as if to confirm my diagnosis.

"Okay, people. Thank you so much for all the help. Listen up for what's going to happen."

It was another voice, this time a tall woman in a bright orange jacket. She wore tall brown leather boots and was walking up and down our line shouting over the sound of the rain. She was from the Missouri Humane Society, and they had just arrived with a horse trailer that was parked along the highway's service road. We were to lead our horses to this trailer and they would be brought to an animal hospital, where they could be treated for their wounds and trauma.

"Once they're all in the trailer, you guys can get back to your cars and get going," she said.

I was tenth in line, but I could see that none of the horses ahead of us were moving. They stood like statues, as if stunned into immovable stone. People clucked and encouraged them, but not a limb stirred.

I looked into the eye of my horse. "Hey," I said. "How about you set an example? What do you say? Will you come with me a little farther?"

With one hand under his chin and the other hand holding the long stringy clump of mane, I swallowed the jittery feeling in my throat and guided him forward out of the line. We turned and walked toward the waiting trailer. All the other horses watched us, and as we passed the last one in line, they slowly turned one by one and followed our lead.

The woman in the orange jacket was waiting at the ramp that led into the trailer. She smiled and thanked me as she grabbed the horse by his whole face and leaned close to his ear.

"Hey, boy," she said quietly. "You're one weary Morgan. I bet you're no more than three years old. We'll get you cleaned up and right as rain." She turned to find me still standing there.

"Thank you, young lady. You go on now, so the others can get in here."

It was only when I was waiting for Aunt Patti to walk back to the car that I started to cry.

chapter

Aunt Patti and I never made it to St. Louis. Even if they hadn't closed the highway for hours, neither of us felt like celebrating after our experience, or explaining to everyone what had happened. Aunt Patti and I were a lot alike in that way, so turning back to Plattsburgh was the obvious thing to do. Sitting side by side in silence, we headed for home. There didn't seem to be anything to say, or anything either of us felt like saying out loud. I knew it might be a long time before I was ready to talk about what had just happened. I had never witnessed anything so bloody and violent before. Maybe it was shock, but I kept thinking about how one second everything was so normal, and then the very next second everything was totally in disaster mode.

Once home, Aunt Patti made us a couple of turkey sandwiches for dinner and we went into the living room to watch TV. Chase climbed up onto the couch next to me so I could scratch his belly. For dessert, Aunt Patti brought out a quart of milk, two glasses, and all the brownies.

"Sometimes the only thing a person can do after a day like this is eat brownies," she said.

I gave a small laugh. This was a private joke of ours, one we always made after something upsetting happened. Sometimes "the only thing a person can do" was eat potato chips, or drink a milk shake, or curl up with Chase and read comic books, or watch *The Princess Diaries* for the millionth time. The whole gist of the joke was that sometimes the only thing you could do to make yourself feel better was exactly what you felt like doing.

Aunt Patti was only thirty-one years old. Like me, she had superthick brown curly hair, but she kept hers chin-length, while mine was long. I usually pulled it back in a messy bun and only brushed it out once a week or so because it was so hard to untangle. Our hair wasn't the only reason people mistook us for mother and daughter. We also had the same brown eyes, which people always described as sparkly. We were both short, and people would comment that neither of us looked our age. Aunt Patti took that as a compliment, but I did not. Aunt Patti joked that one day I would.

Aunt Patti plopped down next to me and poured two tall glasses of milk. We each picked up a thick brownie and took big bites. She took the remote from me and flipped through channels. She stopped when she got to the news.

"Here it is, April."

"Will you please pour me another glass?"

We were riveted by the story, which the newscaster described in detail. The trailer had been passing through Missouri on its way from Oklahoma to a horse-meat-processing plant in DeKalb, Illinois. The crash killed seventeen horses altogether. Twenty-five had survived. The pictures of the accident scene frightened me all over again. I found myself thinking about the horse that I had escorted to the trailer. He was only one of twenty-five. What was happening to him and all the others right now? How did he feel? Could he comprehend what was going on?

The reporter said that dozens of veterinarians and Humane Society volunteers had gathered up the animals and tended to their wounds in the aftermath. It was still unclear, however, what would happen to the animals now. Technically, the slaughterhouse still owned them.

"Who eats horse meat anyway?" I asked.

"*Shhh*. Listen for a sec."

I grabbed another brownie.

"The Humane Society of Missouri immediately opened negotiations with the owner's insurance company," the reporter said as the TV showed pictures of a horse getting its foot bandaged. "Local advocates are hoping that the owner will transfer possession of the survivors to the society in exchange for the Humane Society's agreeing to waive the eighty-four thousand dollars spent on rescuing and treating the animals."

"What does that all mean?" I asked when the segment ended and a car commercial came on.

"It means that maybe instead of going back on the road to the slaughterhouse and being turned into meat, these horses can stay here and be put up for adoption," Aunt Patti said, crumpling her paper napkin and sticking it into her empty milk glass. "Shady Glen Rescue Ranch is just outside of Plattsburgh. It's up off Belleview Road, just a couple miles out of town."

"Is that where the horses are now?" I asked.

"I think so," Aunt Patti replied. "But to answer your other question, April, plenty of people eat horse meat. Just not here in the U.S. This processor supplies the market in Belgium, they said."

"Oh, yeah, I heard someone say that right after the accident. Gross."

"Don't say gross," Aunt Patti said. "And don't make a sour face like that. Some people think eating cows is gross. Other people think eating pigs is gross. Everyone has their own customs and beliefs. Just because we don't do something doesn't make it wrong for everyone."

"I know we're supposed to think that, but I don't know. Some things just seem wrong no matter what."

"Look who's going absolutely horsey," Aunt Patti joked.

"It's not that," I said seriously. I wasn't sure what I meant, so I stopped talking and watched Aunt Patti gather her scrapbooking materials.

Her May topic was "copycat plants." There were certain species of plants that evolved to look like predators so that birds and insects would stay away. Aunt Patti was thinking of devoting a whole section of her flower shop to these sorts of plants.

"Copycat plants would be great to have working for you in a garden," she said, picking up a pamphlet entitled "Mimesis."

I couldn't help rolling my eyes at how nerdy Aunt Patti could be sometimes. Luckily, she was supercool in other ways, letting me do stuff on my own that my friends' parents wouldn't think of letting them do. She said kids shouldn't live as if they were under lock and key.

I picked up the cordless phone, which was stuck between the couch cushions. I called Lowell and left a message for him to call me back as soon as possible. I needed someone else to talk to about the accident.

Plattsburgh is not a big town, but it is big enough to have several different neighborhoods. As a county seat, we have a beautiful brick courthouse right in the center of town among other official buildings, little restaurants, and small shops, like Aunt Patti's Room for Blooms. There are nice homes near the town center, too. I wouldn't say that we lived in the poorest part of town—that would be the trailer park and broken-down houses down along Beakman's Creek, near the lumberyard and DeGregorio's restaurant—but we were definitely not in the richest part, either. Aunt Patti and I lived in a small one-story house on East Hickory. She called it "our humble bungalow." Our house had two bedrooms, a small kitchen, a combined living room/dining room, and a front porch. One whole wall of the living room was lined with bookshelves and filled with the books that had once belonged to my parents. All of Aunt Patti's books were there as well. We had no basement. Plattsburgh is laced with creeks and streams that feed into the Bourbeuse River, so hardly anyone had a basement. The ground was just too wet for too much of the year. Basements tended to flood with groundwater.

When my parents were alive, we lived in a much larger house on the property alongside the stable they managed. After the accident, Aunt Patti said she wanted something much easier to manage and "much, much easier to afford." She was only twenty-two when my parents died and she had just graduated from Mizzou, which is the state university up in Columbia. Her degree was in biology. She had planned to be a science teacher, but then everything changed for her and me both.

After looking around, Aunt Patti settled on 214 East Hickory. The house was small, but it sat on nearly two acres. The house next door had burned down a long time ago and the previous owner combined the lots into one. "Garden-wise, I knew I could sink my teeth into this yard," she once told me. And she did. Aunt Patti grew almost all our vegetables. She was also constantly experimenting, trying out this or that flower or plant to see what kinds of things she could grow from seed. Her most successful experiment resulted in a large plot of buffalo grass, which was native to our area and did better the more we stomped on it. She also created a hybrid tomato whose outer skin was a mixture of golden yellow and red. Sometimes I teased her that she was like a Dr. Frankenstein of plants, which she took as a compliment.

I was so young when we moved into the East Hickory house that I didn't really have anything to compare it to. All in all, it felt like home.

I put the phone down and looked back up at the TV. The weather report was on, which always caught Aunt Patti's attention. Because of her garden, she was obsessed with the weather. Especially then, when all it did was rain.

"Holy cow," she said as the weatherwoman pointed to an unbroken blanket of gray clouds massed all over eastern and central Missouri. There was no sign of it clearing up. "April, this is bad. We're all going to get root rot, not just the garden."

"It has to stop eventually," I said.

"Well, eventually can't come soon enough," she said, turning off the television. "April, I'm exhausted. How about we call it a night?"

As I carried the glasses and brownie plate into the kitchen, I thought about the horse I had helped that afternoon. I pictured the way its sad brown eye had looked at me. Part of me could not believe what I had done. If someone had told me that a day would come when I would get within ten feet of a horse—not to mention touch it, guide it, and feel sorry for it—I would have said "no way." I think Aunt Patti must have read my mind, because she came up to me in the kitchen and put her arm around my shoulders.

"You were some kind of hero this afternoon," she said. "I'm proud of you."

"Thanks," I said. "But it just sort of happened. In a way, it doesn't feel like the person who did that was me. Before today, if somebody had asked me to get a huge horse into a trailer I would have said I couldn't."

"That's right. But you're not the first person who did something she thought she couldn't. Sometimes the only way we know we can do something is by doing it. Act first, think later."

"But that's the opposite of STAR."

Aunt Patti looked at me questioningly. "STAR?"

"You know," I said, "S-T-A-R—Stop, Think, Act, and Reflect. What we learned in fourth grade when all the boys were constantly getting into fistfights."

Aunt Patti laughed and kissed the top of my head. "I guess sometimes, like today, it's more like A-S-T-R—Act, Stop, Think, Reflect. Go brush your teeth and get ready for bed."

On the way to my room I passed the living room bookcase. Usually I avoided paying attention to the books there, but that night I stopped and read the titles on the spines. There were dozens of books, but four caught my eye. *The Black Stallion, To Race a Dream, Misty of Chincoteague, Black Beauty*. They were my mom's old horse books, the ones she had read as a girl. I had always resented those books. I figured that if she had never read them, she wouldn't have loved horses as much as she did. And if she had not loved horses, she wouldn't have died. But things were different now. For the first time, I wondered which came first, the love of horses or the books?

I made sure that Aunt Patti was out of sight in the kitchen before I pulled *Black Beauty* off the shelf. I hurried to my room and tucked the book under my covers. Then I washed up, shouted out good night, and jumped into bed. The rain tapped steadily on the roof overhead.

chapter

Black Beauty, the Autobiography of a Horse. The cover, title, and illustrations all looked old-fashioned, like a book from another era. I opened to the first page and started reading. Black Beauty was actually the narrator. It had been years since I had read anything told from the point of view of an animal and at first it seemed like an immature way of telling a story. But the picture at the top of the page was so peaceful—a horse dipping its head into a pond to drink, with a full leafy tree right behind him—that I kept going. What did I care if it was babyish? Nobody could see me.

> *The first place that I can well remember was a large pleasant meadow with a pond of clear water in it . . .*
>
> *While I was young I lived upon my mother's milk, as I could not eat grass. In the daytime I ran by her side, and at night I lay down close by her. When it was hot, we used to stand by the pond in the shade of the trees, and when it was cold, we had a nice warm shed near the plantation.*

I read for an hour, lost in a totally different world. Suddenly I heard Aunt Patti call out to me.

"April?"

"Yeah?"

"You're still up? I see your light's still on."

"I know."

"I think you ought to call it a day."

"In a sec."

"Good night, hon."

"Good night."

I turned back to the yellowing pages of the open book. Black Beauty's mother was giving him advice, the thing she wanted him to remember after he got sold.

> *I hope you will fall into good hands; but a horse never knows who will buy him, or who may drive him; it is all a chance for us, but still I say, do your best wherever it is, and keep up your good name.*

I closed the book and put it on my nightstand. I turned out the light and shut my eyes. Maybe because I was really tired, or just plain out of it, I had to remind myself that Black Beauty's mother didn't really exist, nor did she pass along those words of wisdom. She was a horse, for heaven's sake! And of course it was corny advice anyway—all that business about doing your best and keeping up your good name—but at the same time the words did make me think. A person is born to parents but never has a say about who those parents are. All of us just fall into hands. I, for one, fell into the hands of my mother and father, and then "chance" took me away from them, or them away from me. After that, I had no say about what happened. This was something I had never really thought about before. Where would I be if there had been no Aunt Patti?

Sunday morning I woke up ravenous. I raised my blinds and saw that it was still raining, but at least not too hard. Normally on Sundays Aunt Patti and I blasted a CD and made something special—pancakes, waffles, or omelettes. But that day felt different from the start. I shuffled into the kitchen to find Aunt Patti at the table reading the paper.

"Hey," I said.

"Morning," she said, looking up and smiling, her eyes back to their bright, cheerful look.

"Is that the story about the accident?" I asked, moving behind her chair so I could see the pictures. I retied my tangled mess of a bun so my hair would quit blocking my view.

"Mm-hmm. Turns out one of those survivors is pregnant. Another one is a stallion, a Thoroughbred originally from Kentucky." She took a sip of coffee. "How these animals got to Oklahoma to be sold for meat, I don't understand."

Times may be different from when *Black Beauty* was written, but the same question had bothered me the night before. It seemed so awful to be bought and sold, separated from family and friends over and over again throughout your life and have no say about any of it. Black Beauty and all the other horses just accepted it as a matter of fact— they were dependent on human masters and had to go wherever they were told.

Who was the horse I had helped? Where did he come from? How did he wind up on that horrible ride to the slaughterhouse? And what would happen to him now? I remembered his sad eye and his soft hair. How strong his muscles felt when, leading him to the trailer, I pressed against the warm, wet weight of his flank.

"I don't get it, either," I said.

"Your parents would be beside themselves. Furious. Your mom, especially. She refused to stable a horse if she didn't like the way an owner treated it. I know for a fact that she drove away more than one client," Aunt Patti said. "But you must be hungry and I'm just sitting here. Let's eat."

We had French toast with syrup. It tasted good but my mind was whirling.

"Aunt Patti?"

"Yeah?"

"Do you think we could go over to the rescue ranch and see what's going on, I mean see whether they need any help or anything?"

Aunt Patti put down her fork and stared at me. I looked down at my plate and hoped she wouldn't call attention to my having a change of heart about horses. I really did not want to have to explain myself, mostly because I didn't think that I *could*.

Thank goodness she let it go.

"I'll give a call after breakfast," she said.

Just then the phone rang and I jumped up from the table to answer. It was Lowell.

"Hey, I got your message," he said, his voice sounding bland. "What's up?"

"Hey, not much. Actually, a lot. Aunt Patti and I were on our way into St. Louis yesterday when that accident happened on Fifty-four."

"You mean the one with the horses?" Instantly Lowell's voice didn't sound quite so bored. I checked that Aunt Patti was engrossed in the newspaper and drifted out to the living room where she wouldn't hear me.

"Yeah. And this one horse, well, I don't know. This one horse was pretty cool."

"Pretty cool how?"

"Well, I was just standing by our car when he came up from behind me," I said.

"What'd you do?"

"At first I freaked out, but then I led it over to this trailer they had set up."

Lowell didn't say anything, but then again, I didn't expect him to.

"Anyway, I gotta go," I said. "I'll see you."

"Wait. April?"

"Yeah?"

"Then what happened?"

Now it was the old Lowell speaking, the pre-angry Lowell. That was all I needed to hear.

"Well, I don't really know how I did it, but it was like I had a connection with that horse. His face was all bloody and he looked so sad and beaten down. I felt like I could have led him anywhere. I got him to walk up this ramp into the trailer and all the other survivor horses followed him. It sounds crazy, but now I feel like I've got to see him again. I was just asking Aunt Patti about it. All the survivors were taken over to Shady Glen."

There was a long silence on the phone.

"Lowell? Are you there?"

"I'm here. I was just thinking. It doesn't sound crazy at all."

Winding northwest from Plattsburgh, the uphill road to Shady Glen Rescue Ranch passes a small wooden church with an overgrown cemetery. There we turned left and descended into a grassy valley. The ranch had three or four corrals, two stables, an administration building, and an outdoor picnic area covered by a tin roof. Five or six cars and pickup trucks were parked around the main stable. The rain had stopped, but the sky was still thick and gray. As Aunt Patti pulled into a slot, I looked out my window and saw an enormous pink pig nosing in the mud. Another pig, this one brown and smaller, walked freely in the tall weeds alongside a dirt road.

As we climbed out of the car, an older woman in overalls and boots came out of a door in the stable. She was the person who had been directing the rescue yesterday on I-54. She was carrying the same clipboard.

"Miss Helmbach?" she said to Aunt Patti.

"That's me, but please call me Patti. And this is my niece, April. April Helmbach."

We all shook hands.

"I'm Leigh Fort. I remember you, April. You had that chestnut gelding, the one that climbed into the trailer first. You handled him like an old pro."

I didn't know whether to tell Leigh that when it came to horses, I was the furthest thing from an old pro. Before I could say anything, a tiny man came bursting out of the big stable door. He wasn't much taller than me, and I'm only five foot one. The man had huge hands, and his arms from the elbow down were as thick as my thighs. On his way out, he tripped over a stone, swore at it, and glared as if the rock had intended to trip him.

"Excuse me, ladies," he said.

Leigh laughed and introduced us.

"Marty, this is April and Patti Helmbach. Patti, April, this is Marty Smitherman."

"Hi," Aunt Patti and I chirped in unison.

"There is nothing about horses that Marty doesn't know from firsthand experience," Leigh informed us.

"Did you say Helmbach?" Marty asked Leigh. He was looking at me.

"I did."

"I knew your folks," he said. "We went back a ways, your mom and dad and me. I had a lot of respect for those two and what they were trying to do. It's not easy boarding horses, doing what you know is right. And it's even harder trying to convince owners that what you say is right *is* right."

I was speechless. I was always taken aback when I met someone who knew my parents. Whoever it was had a window into my life—into *me*—that I had not known existed.

"Wow," Aunt Patti said.

"You probably don't remember," he said, still looking at me, "but when your mom and dad were working, I used to watch you toddle around the barn with a currycomb in one hand and a hoof pick in the other."

"A hoof pick?" I asked. "A currycomb? I'm guessing those were baby toys of some sort?"

Marty looked incredulous. He turned to Leigh. "This is April Helmbach, right? Daughter of Mary Beth and Harry Helmbach?"

I had no time to get offended by Marty's sarcasm because just then we all heard a piercing whinny from inside the barn. The sound terrified me.

"Someone in there wants attention," Marty said.

Without meaning to, I inched closer to Aunt Patti. Marty noticed me do this and looked even more puzzled.

"Follow me," he told us.

chapter

The barn was airy and light. Big stable doors stood open at each end, allowing the moist May air to flow inside. Even on a gray day, the high ceiling and open windows at every stall made it seem cheery. The air smelled of freshly cut wood, sawdust, bandages, and manure. I also smelled something sharp, which I soon realized came from the disinfectant and antibiotic creams people were applying to the horses' wounds. It was a smell I recognized from the vet's office, when we took Chase for his shots.

Ahead of us, a long black head peered over a stall door and watched us enter. As we got closer, I could see that two people were attending to the horse. While one person changed a bandage on a rear leg, the other rubbed the horse's side with a red rubber thing that looked like a spiky soap dish. Horses and people filled stalls; everyone seemed to be performing a treatment of some sort. Every so often you heard a horse whinny, nicker, or blow out through his lips. Then you heard a human voice respond something like, "Okay, I know, we're almost done."

Tucked behind one low wall was a group of ducks and hens. Leigh noticed me looking at the birds.

"We don't only rescue horses," she said. "We get reports from all over the state if someone's not taking proper care of an animal. Whatever the animal."

"Why don't they?" I asked. "Take proper care, I mean."

"You'd be surprised. Some people just run out of money and stop feeding them. Other people are hoarders and don't know when to stop accumulating all kinds of stuff, including animals. We've got pigs, goats, ponies, emus, and even a llama. And that was before all these guys came in last night!" She swept her arm through the air. "Thank goodness for the volunteers or we'd be overwhelmed."

Aunt Patti and Marty had wandered over to pet a small horse shaking his head above the half-wall of his stall. Aunt Patti was talking to Marty quietly. I had a feeling they were talking about me so I turned away. Leigh took a call on her cell phone and raised a finger to tell me that she would just be a minute.

Still standing just inside the barn door, I didn't know what to do with myself. I could hear the sounds of horses—whinnies, nickers, neighs, stamps, and snorts— and I started to get panicky again. I closed my eyes and took a deep breath. Even though my eyes were still closed,

I saw a glowing orange ball. Then the ball got smaller and I realized that it was the sun—a warm sun dipping down behind some evergreen trees—just as if I was looking out a western-facing window at the end of the day. In front of the trees, almost right under my nose, I saw a wooden ledge like a windowsill. Hanging off of it was a dented bucket full of grain and a second undented bucket of water. Below the buckets, two long, straight, velvety brown legs stood very still in the straw.

"April? You want to go on a tour?" It was Leigh. I opened my eyes and saw her approach. "Your aunt Patti and Marty are catching up on old times."

She smiled and pointed deeper into the barn.

"Let's see if we can find the chestnut who found you yesterday. I think he's just around the corner here."

Two swallows swooped down from a nest high up in the rafters and fluttered out the main door behind me. I walked beside Leigh, looking left and right at the caretakers and the accident survivors.

"How did you recruit all these volunteers?" I asked.

"Well, for that we can thank the television and news reports. Word got out and people came in droves. You'd be surprised how many people contacted us to see if they could help. We had to turn away about a dozen volunteers."

We turned right at the end of the center aisle of the barn and walked along the western row of stalls. Somehow, without knowing which stall I was bound for, I stopped at the third one and looked in.

I was shocked to find that the stall matched exactly the image that had appeared behind my closed eyes just moments ago. The western view, the evergreens, the ledge, the buckets, the brown legs—it was all the same. The only difference was that the sun wasn't setting. And there he was—the horse who found me the day before. Our eyes met like old friends. There was no blood on his face today, only the dark stitches that had closed his cut. Both eyes were open, and his bangs had been washed and combed, revealing a white diamond-shaped marking on his forehead. For a moment it was like we were not meeting as two different species. We were simply beings whose lives had intertwined like the strands of a braided rope. It struck me that this horse and I were meant to find each other. If not, how could I have pre-imagined what I would find there in the Shady Glen stall?

"Hi again," I said to the gelding.

Leigh came over and stroked his nose. "This guy's a sweetie. You're an old soldier, aren't you, boy? You and April showed everybody that it was okay to walk right back into a trailer, didn't you?"

"What's his name?" I asked.

Leigh laughed.

"Honey, we've spent the last fifteen hours patching, stitching, tending, and nursing these horses. A day ago they were well on their way to becoming steaks."

Even though Leigh was joking, what she said didn't strike me as all that funny. "We haven't gotten around to naming them yet," she added.

"Rainy Day." The name popped out of my mouth.

"Rainy Day?" Leigh asked.

"Would that be okay?"

"I don't see why not. Every day is a rainy day this year. Looks like we've got ourselves a Morgan called Rainy Day. I'll tell the others."

Leigh's cell phone rang again. "April," she said, moving away from me, "I've got to get this. How'd you like to spend a minute or two comforting Rainy Day? We're trying to reassure the horses who've already received the medical care they needed. From now on, it's all about building trust. With some of them, we'll have a long way to go."

"Sure." My voice was steady, but I was nervous to the core. Leigh walked away talking.

I looked at Rainy Day. He swung his head over to my hand and took a step in my direction. He was completely dry now, unlike yesterday, so the heat of his body came straight into my palm and up my whole arm. I smiled. The longer I patted him, exploring his whole face, neck, and whiskery chin with both hands, the less afraid I felt. It was like a big block of ice deep inside me was slowly melting. Rainy Day was watching me. He kept shifting his head so that he could look at me with one eye and then the other.

"You're probably wondering what happens now," I said. "All I know is it seems like you and your friends here have gotten a second chance."

Maybe, in a way, I had, too.

chapter

6

I lost track of time and was startled when Leigh, Aunt Patti, and Marty came up behind me. Rainy Day blew air out of his lips, grunted, and shook his head.

"Well, look at you," Leigh said.

"This gal has horses in her blood," Marty said, laying a heavy hand across my shoulders. "Anyone can see that. From what I hear, she's been a fish out of water."

Aunt Patti and I looked at each other but I said nothing. Obviously, Aunt Patti and Marty *had* been talking about me. Was it true? Had I been missing out all these years? Did I really belong in barns and alongside horses like my parents? If so, how could I get back in the water, as Marty would say? As far as I could tell, there was only one way—jump into the deep end and swim.

"Leigh," I said, "what happens to these horses now? I mean, once they're healed. Will they live here? Can people adopt them the way they adopt dogs and cats?"

Leigh reached over to pat Rainy Day. "Well, first we have to make sure this deal with the owner's insurance people comes through and the animals have been transferred to us. After that, the Humane Society has a couple of ways of handling the larger animals. Some people will donate money for us to keep the horses here. Other people, those with working farms, come in and adopt the traditional way—they take them home. This guy isn't in bad shape at all. He would be ready to go in a couple of days, if we could find him the right place."

"Aunt Patti?" I started, but she interrupted before I could say more.

"Honey, I think I know what you're going to say. But it's too soon and I think maybe your feelings are running away with you. We had a traumatic experience of our own, too, yesterday. It's natural for you to feel attached to this guy—"

"Rainy Day," I blurted, already defensive.

"Rainy Day, excuse me. It's natural for you to feel attached, but life is more complicated than that. I understand you wanting to visit, and I even think I understand why you have your personal reasons to want to bond with—"

"Pardon me, Patti," Marty said. "Where do you and April live? I lost touch with the family after her parents after the accident."

Warily, Aunt Patti described our tiny house and our huge yard. Yes, it was fenced, she told him. Completely fenced with old post and rail. I waited and listened. It seemed to me that Rainy Day—standing very still—listened, too. Marty asked what had been done with all the stuff that had belonged to my parents—the tack, the supplies, the blankets, the hoses, and the tools.

"Marty, that was nine years ago." Aunt Patti sighed. "I was practically a girl myself. We put everything from the house and the stable into storage. The rest of the family and I figured it should be April's decision what to do with all their things when she was old enough."

They all looked at me but this time I kept my mouth shut. It was the first I had ever heard about equipment, furniture, or any of the things that had belonged to my parents.

"Let's back up here," Marty continued. "April, what is it you were going to say before? Could be we've all jumped the gun."

"You didn't jump the gun," I said. "I was going to ask if we could adopt Rainy Day. But what Aunt Patti just said distracted me." I turned to her accusingly.

"Why didn't you ever tell me about all that equipment and stuff?"

"I guess there just never seemed to be a good time to bring it up," she said, looking at me. "You were always so afraid of horses, but I didn't feel right getting rid of all the supplies they'd accumulated, in case someday things changed. I wanted you to be able to make those decisions when you were older."

Aunt Patti put her arm around my shoulder and went on.

"The closest I came was moving all your mom's books into the house with us. Not that you ever looked at them. I guess I thought they ought to be in view just in case. But this is all beside the point, April. We don't have the skill or the expertise. We don't even have a barn!"

"Maybe I can help you with that," Marty said. "Of course, it's not my decision, but I could come around if you ever needed backup. I could get a little prefab barn set up in no time at all, and it sounds like you have what you need to make a safe paddock."

"But April doesn't know the first thing about taking care of a horse. Until yesterday it didn't look like she would ever want to, either. And I'm not in any position to do anything. I've got the business to run and April to care for. I just can't see—"

"I can take care of that, too," Marty said. "You know

I'm right here in Plattsburgh. April's thirteen years old. At no charge to you, I can get a smart, willing, and capable girl taking care of a horse in no time. What you two need to decide is whether or not April is all those things."

Aunt Patti never stood a chance. She raised a few more objections, but they got weaker and weaker every time Marty and I weighed in with a counterargument. The truth is, I don't think I could have convinced her if Marty hadn't been there, too. He was on my side from the start.

A little while later we left Shady Glen. We told Leigh that we would return for Rainy Day when his health was stable and we had our place ready for him.

"It'll be a hastier adoption than we like," Leigh said. "But this is clearly an unusual set of circumstances. I really can't think of anything better for Rainy Day or for April."

My only worry as we left was whether Rainy Day would be happy with me. What if he sensed that I was too inexperienced to take care of him? Was I really the same little girl who Marty had watched toddle around a barn with those grooming tools?

As soon as we pulled up to the house, Lowell appeared at our front door. He must have been watching from his window.

"Hi there, Lowell," Aunt Patti said. "Stay for lunch."

"Hey, Lowell," I said, smiling to think I would have another ally. I knew Aunt Patti still had mixed feelings about Rainy Day coming to live with us, and without Leigh or Marty around I wondered whether I would be able to keep up the fight. Lowell's presence broke the tension in the room. Aunt Patti plopped down in a kitchen chair and took off her glasses to wipe them with a paper napkin.

"I'll get lunch together in a sec," she said as I signaled silently to Lowell to not say anything just yet.

Over grilled cheese sandwiches and carrot sticks, I told him about the accident and our trip to Shady Glen.

"So you're going to have a new neighbor," I said. "A four-legged neighbor."

Lowell laughed and squeezed more ketchup onto his plate. He always dipped his grilled cheese in ketchup.

"Lowell," Aunt Patti said, "I want you to talk some sense into your friend here. Chase, stop begging off Lowell."

Aunt Patti smiled, so I knew she wasn't seriously upset, but I was concerned that she seemed to think there was still room for changing her mind. Lowell crunched on a carrot stick and passed a piece of his sandwich crust to Chase under the table. Aunt Patti pretended not to notice and waited until Lowell caught her eye.

"It's one thing to get over a longtime fear of horses. I've

wanted April to do that for years. But adopting a horse of her own is going too far in the other direction, don't you think?"

I didn't give him a chance to answer. Aunt Patti and I were treating Lowell like a wall, bouncing our opinions off him so we wouldn't have to bounce them off each other.

"Lowell, this guy Marty, a trainer who knew my parents, said he'd teach me everything I need to know for free. Besides, I must have picked up something in my first four years. He said he used to watch me toddle around barns with some sort of horse gadgets—I forget what he called them—in my hands. I know I can do this," I said confidently.

Silence. Lowell took a long sip of an orange sports drink he found in our fridge. Aunt Patti and I both expected him to say something profound and decisive.

"A horse would be awesome," Lowell said.

That was profound and decisive enough for me! I could have hugged him.

After lunch Lowell and I went outside even though it was wet and soggy. We walked all the way around my yard. Even while we talked, I kept picturing Rainy Day standing around eating grass, the same way Black Beauty had looked in that picture.

Just like we used to do, Lowell and I wound up by his play set and I climbed onto the double swing. Although I'm short, my knees still popped up too high for me to really pump. Lowell wedged his wide bottom into the normal swing but he didn't move. He sat with a long stick in his hand, poking at the stony ground. Neither of us said anything about how long it had been since we had really talked.

"Thanks for that," I said. "I mean, for taking my side about adopting Rainy Day."

"Don't mention it. It really *will* be awesome."

"I think so, too," I said. "So what's up with you?"

Lowell drew a circle in the dirt and I watched his cheerfulness disappear. I was afraid he wouldn't answer me, or that he'd answer with his sullen shrug. But that wasn't it at all. Lowell had been so down on everything and everyone, it was like he didn't know where to begin. His dad was home too much, yelling all the time. When his mom was at work, his dad hung out at this bar in St. Clair. Lowell knew his dad was suffering over not finding work, but he couldn't understand why he took that frustration out on his own family.

"I know he's pissed or whatever, and ashamed and frustrated and embarrassed. And I do feel sorry for him,"

Lowell said, "but sometimes I get so mad I could just…So I end up staying in my room." Lowell stabbed at a rock with the stick. "Why can't he just admit that things have changed and that he'll have to go do something else?"

"Maybe that's too hard for him right now," I said.

"Plus, I suck at sports," Lowell said. "That drives my dad crazy, too. You have no idea how lousy life is for a guy who sucks at sports, April."

"You're right. I don't."

"I feel like crawling into a hole and coming out when I'm twenty-one."

"Hey, twenty-one might not be any better," I joked. "Seriously, remember you're not alone. I'm here if you ever want to talk."

"Yeah," he said. "Thanks. A person can always use a place to rant."

To my huge relief, he smiled.

I went home and spent the rest of the day doing chores and homework. When I was done with that, I read more of *Black Beauty*. Black Beauty was off on his own now and meeting all kinds of other horses. One of them was named Ginger. All the humans thought she was difficult and dangerous, but that was only because she had been roughly trained and treated. Her mouth was in pain all the time from wearing the worst kind of bit. Compared to Ginger, Black Beauty felt lucky, even when he was nearly killed by a young groom who didn't know not to give him cold water to drink after a long hard run. One scene after another showed Black Beauty dealing with the consequences of people doing incredibly stupid things. I had never given much thought to any of this before, but *Black Beauty* made me see the horse's point of view. People did do incredibly stupid things, things that made others—especially kids and animals—suffer.

Aunt Patti and I had dinner early. We were both worn out. Later on, as I was brushing my teeth, she stopped by the bathroom. I looked at her face behind mine in the mirror.

"April, Marty called. He said you're welcome to stop by his stable tomorrow morning before school for your first day of training."

"Before school?" I said, my mouth full of foamy toothpaste.

"He said six A.M."

"And what did you say?"

"I said, 'If I can get that girl out of bed at five-thirty in the morning, you're welcome to her.'"

I spat, rinsed, and gave Aunt Patti a huge hug.

chapter

A blue haze filled all the low-lying pockets of Plattsburgh at five-thirty the next morning. If I hadn't been so tired, I would have said something about how beautiful the world looked, as if the mist were protecting the earth overnight until the sun came up to warm the ground. I had never known how magical dawn could be.

When Aunt Patti had woken me up, I could barely open my eyes. It was too early to eat anything, but I managed to drink some orange juice before shoveling myself into clothes. I remembered to pull on old jeans and work boots like Marty had suggested. Somehow I braided my hair and stuffed shorts and flip-flops into my backpack for school later on. Aunt Patti dropped me at the entrance to the stable and drove away.

I heard the sound of a hose filling a bucket and headed in that direction. Marty was stirring something brown and grainy into the water when I called out to him.

"Hey!"

"You made it," he said, his voice deep and calm. "A

good sign." He walked toward me and grasped my hand, enclosing the whole thing in his enormous grip. We stood eye to eye.

A brown-and-white horse stuck its head out of the stall and looked at me.

"That's Venus," Marty said, cocking his head toward the horse. "She's the top banana around here. I'm going to introduce you to her first, because once you've got Venus on your side, you got it made. Follow me, April."

Marty took Venus by the chin and rubbed her nose, her jaws, and between her ears.

"Venus, say hello to April. April, let her smell the back of your hand. That's what I always want you to do when you meet a new horse. And be calm. Very calm. Horses notice every gesture and every sound you make, so you never want to do or say anything to make them feel afraid."

I did what Marty said. Venus's ears flicked around and faced every which way like rotating satellite dishes. She turned her head so she was looking directly at me.

"The most important thing to remember," Marty said, "is that while these animals may look and seem like big tough guys, that's not how they think of themselves. What they think they are is prey. They think like prey and they act like prey."

"What do you mean?"

"I mean, see that? See the way her ears moved around the second you spoke? She hadn't ever heard your voice before. It's new to her, and she needs to figure out whether you're safe or dangerous. Horses are constantly assessing their environments with all their senses—smell, sight, sound, taste, touch, and of course intuition. The littlest unexpected situation can send them into a panic. They're more like a rabbit or a deer than a...than a..."

"T. rex?"

Marty laughed. "Exactly. You get the picture."

"What do they do when they panic?" I asked.

"What do deer do?"

"Run?"

"Exactly. They'll run, or if they can't run they'll rear, shriek, or any number of other unpleasant things."

All this time, Marty was rubbing Venus all over and keeping his voice low. He paused, and Venus snorted out a spray that landed on my hand. I flinched.

"I guess stepping into a nest of yellow jackets would count as especially scary," I said, watching Venus shake her head. Part of me wanted to get Marty to talk about my parents, but I was afraid that if I looked him in the eye I might start to choke up.

"Mmm…" Marty said. "That was a terrible thing," he said quietly. "Never saw anything like it before or since."

I nodded, fighting back a buried rage. I hated that a complete fluke stole my parents from me. If there had been no yellow jackets, if that filly had not stepped right on them, if my mom had managed to hold on, if those hooves hadn't landed just so . . .

A few more horses stuck their heads out and nickered softly.

"Is that breakfast?" I asked, indicating the brown stuff in the bucket at our feet, carefully changing the subject.

"This? This is a brown mash I had to make up for one of our geldings. He's had a bad stomach for a week and I'm trying to get it straightened out. His owner's worried and wants to bring in the vet. The others will just get some fresh hay and oats, and of course clean water. Come on, let's get to the chores. Chores and horses go together."

I tagged along with Marty and followed his instructions—I watched when he told me to watch, and helped when he told me to help. We went inside the stable, which was warm and lit with bare electric bulbs that dangled from the ceiling. He handed me an oval-shaped piece of plastic, the soap-dish like tool I remembered from Shady Glen, and a bristle brush.

"This is a currycomb," he explained, indicating the plastic tool. "I want you to go brush a horse named Left Bank all over—one pass with the currycomb and one with the regular brush. The curry gets the dirt off her coat and the brush makes her hair smooth. Remember, let her get to know you first, and begin on the left side. Talk to her quietly. No sudden sounds or gestures. Routine, routine, routine, April. Always do everything the same way in the same order every single day. Makes it easy, in a way—you don't forget what you have to do. And watch you don't get stepped on."

Stepped on! Just the sound of that phrase reminded me of what I had always feared—first a crushing pain, then a shattered foot. My mouth went dry.

"Who and where is Left Bank?"

"Down in the last stall on the left. She's perfectly friendly. A little gray mare with white socks. Belongs to a girl from Chesterfield."

Marty must have noticed something about the look on my face.

"No worries with Left Bank, April. Just routine cleanup. She's easy and good on her feet and won't bother you. I'm sorry if I scared you."

I shook my head no and walked to the last stall to

introduce myself to Left Bank. She was smaller than I expected; her head was at the level of my shoulder. Standing on her left side, I put my hand by her muzzle and said hello. Her nose was pink and her nostrils flared open and closed constantly. Under long eyelashes, her straightforward gaze seemed to be trying to figure out who I was.

"My name's April," I said quietly, suddenly feeling like a waitress. "And I'll be your groomer this morning. Our specials today include the currycomb and the brush."

It helped to think of Left Bank as a nervous restaurant customer, needing friendly service every step of the way. I relaxed and began grooming the way Marty had instructed, a long swirl with the comb followed by a gentle but firm brushing. As short as I am, I was surprised by how easy it was to reach over her back with the comb and brush. The only sounds I heard were a muffled country music song from a radio Marty had on and the occasional stamp of a hoof in the straw bedding of the stalls. It was so peaceful, I lost track of time.

"April," Marty said, "I think you've been working on that horse long enough. We've got fifteen others around here that need attention."

"Oh, sorry. Here I come. See you, Left Bank. Don't

worry about leaving a tip. It was my pleasure to serve you."

Before heading into another stall, I looked at all the supplies down at the end of the stable. All along the wall, on every available peg, I saw harnesses, bridles, halters, ropes, and tools of various shapes and sizes. Combs and brushes sat on shelves, and there was a container of metal tools that looked like bottle openers. Blankets and saddles lay draped over freestanding wooden racks. Posters nailed to the wall displayed detailed information about horses. I took a step closer and read about cleaning horse teeth, bridling, and training. Another poster displayed the breeds of horse, types of saddles, and several ways of knotting rodeo rope. There was a whole overwhelming world of information that I knew nothing about. I was concentrating so hard on the posters that I didn't hear Marty approach behind me.

"What's up?" he asked.

"I can't believe how much I have to learn. Kids my age who are into horses already know everything. I don't think I can ever catch up. I've been afraid for so long, I'll never be the kind of horse person you are, or that…"

"Or that what?"

"Or that my parents were," I said.

Marty looked at me seriously before he replied.

"You don't have to be like me," he said reassuringly. "Or like your parents. You just have to be the horse person that you want to be. And knowing how much you need to learn means you're on the right track. I'd be worried if you came sashaying in here thinking you were good to go, that you just imagined yourself a born trainer who had nothing to learn."

"Ha! As if," I said.

"That's what I mean," Marty said. "The wise person knows that she doesn't know everything." He flipped over a bucket and sat down on top of it. "Sit down for a second, April. Right there, on the bench."

I took a seat.

"What do you remember about your parents?"

I thought for a moment. It was hard to know if the things I remembered were actual memories or scenes implanted in my mind by photographs I had seen. In my mind's eye, I could see a little version of myself sitting in a saddle in front of my mom and waving, but there was a picture of me doing exactly that on my grandmother's dressing table in St. Louis. In another picture, I'm sitting between my parents at a picnic table in the country some-place. I have a big piece of watermelon and I'm jamming the red juicy part into my mouth. Did I remember these experiences or did I only know them because of the pictures? Could I think of an honest-to-goodness memory? Nothing was coming and I shook my head.

"Well, I can tell you something," Marty said. "I once spent a whole night with you and your mother in a freezing barn. A mare was struggling to foal. The foal wasn't lined up the way it was supposed to be—one of the two front legs was lying wrong—and we'd called the vet. The roads were bad on account of snow and he was having a heck of a time getting over to Plattsburgh. You couldn't have been more than six months old. Your father was away, and the only way Mary Beth could make it work was to bring you along. She bundled you up so much that the only part of you we could see were your tiny bright brown eyes. She put you down in a pile of straw right next to her, and she and I stayed right by that mare, comforting her, for three hours straight. Around four in the morning, you woke up and Mary Beth nursed you right there in that barn. I'll never forget it."

"Was the foal okay?"

"She came out fine, with a little help, of course. And you were fine, too, but too little to remember. Now, come on, we've got to get up and get going. There's one more thing I want to do with you this morning before I send you packing off to learn about linear equations and the Boston Tea Party."

It was hard to concentrate after the story Marty told. Was that baby in the barn really me?

But I had no time to think about it, because the next thing I knew, Marty was leading a horse over to me. It was small and brown and wore a blue halter. Marty had one hand on the coiled rope and the other hand on the bottom band of the halter under the horse's chin.

"Here," he said. "Lead this guy out into the ring over there."

I started to protest.

"You can do it, April. Look straight ahead, not at him. He's supposed to follow you. You're the leader and he has to know that. Remember to breathe. Atta girl."

We spent a half hour with that horse, whose name turned out to be Grapevine. Marty made me talk to Grapevine as I walked him in all different directions— forward and backward, left and right. He had me start and stop more times than I could count.

Finally, at Marty's direction, I walked Grapevine back to his stall, took off his halter, and brushed him. I filled his rack with fresh hay and hosed water into his bucket. Apart from telling me what to do, Marty hadn't said much after sharing the story about me and my mom on that cold night. Still, I could tell he was pleased.

Aunt Patti pulled up at 7:45 sharp to drive me to school. Marty tapped me gently on my back.

"Thanks for the help," he said. "Tomorrow you ride."

School came and went that day without a single linear equation. When the bell rang at three o'clock, I dashed out and headed straight home. The library wasn't far from my house, just on the other side of Route 50, but it was too far to walk. The first thing I did at home was let Chase out. Then, standing at the back door watching him sniff around under a sky darkening with clouds, I ate a handful of chips and chugged a grape sports drink. I rinsed off my hands and called Chase back in. He went straight to his water bowl and lapped noisily. Before riding off on my bike, I left a note for Aunt Patti saying that I'd be home by six o'clock. I grabbed my poncho and went out the back door.

From the backyard I could see into Lowell's unlit room. He was already home from school and hunched over his keyboard, tapping away by the glow of his screen. I thought about asking him to come with me to the library, but then I heard his parents yelling at each other. It was depressing and worrisome to see Lowell all by himself in the middle of that situation, but I didn't want to knock on their door during a fight. Actually, I was more and more concerned about Lowell spending so much time cooped up in his room at the computer all by himself. In a way, the computer was letting him run away from home without actually leaving. I pushed my bike out from under the overhang by our back door and pedaled off to the library.

The Plattsburgh Library was the main branch of the whole county system. Built only a few years ago on the west side of Route 50, the building was modern and clean. It had automatic glass doors, wide tables for working, and six or seven computers that anyone could use. I went straight to the front desk, where one of the librarians, an older woman with gray hair and a pale face, asked if she could help.

"I'm looking for books about horses," I said hopefully.

"Hmm . . . fiction? Nonfiction? History?" she replied, smiling. "Can you give me a little more direction?"

"Well, I guess I'm looking for books that tell you what horses need and how to take care of them. But also books about horses in general—I mean, what they're like."

"Ah, I see. Information books—nonfiction. Let's go this way."

I followed her past the toddler reading area, where five beanbag chairs were plopped around a colorful carpet.

Near a tiny wooden rocker was a big sign propped against an easel that announced story time that afternoon. *Fairy Tales for Fun*, the sign said. *Happily Ever After Required.* I rolled my eyes at the lame humor you always saw on cutesy homemade signs like that. It was the kind of joke that adults thought little kids liked.

At the other end of the main floor, the librarian stopped.

"Here are the horse books," she said. "While you're looking, I'll check the computer. If we don't have what you need in this building, some other branch in the system might. We can always file a request from St. Louis County."

I squatted down because all the books with the word *horse* in the title seemed to be on the bottom shelves. A couple of books practically jumped into my hand: *Complete Guide to Horse Care* and *Today's Horse*. They were big and fat and packed with all the technical information I would need to learn about keeping a horse. But then a few other titles caught my eye: *Language Without Words: What Horses Mean*, and *Open Channels*. I sat all the way down on the floor and started leafing through them.

According to *Open Channels*, horses and other animals actually communicate with people. Some people used the word *intuition* for this phenomenon. One book explained that intuition was almost like a sixth sense and that most people were born with it. Intuition was an ability to perceive meaning without words. Without knowing a single word, a baby knows the feelings and attitudes of his mother. Little kids often seem able to understand what animals are trying to communicate. And pets can almost always tell when their owners are sad or upset. So far that made sense to me. Sometimes when I collapsed on my bed in a state of total stress, Chase would jump up next to me as if to cheer me up.

Eventually, the book explained, kids pick up from adults that communication needs words, and they stop perceiving the messages they once saw, heard, or sensed coming from the natural world. This didn't have to happen, though. With practice, a person could remain open to intuition. Animal communicators did exactly that: They kept themselves available to exchanging thoughts and feelings with the nonhuman living world. Part of this came from observing and interpreting body language, but there was more to intuition than understanding that a wagging tail meant a dog was happy and that ears pinned back meant a horse was angry.

I looked up at the buzzing white fluorescent light overhead. I had always thought of intuition as a hunch that something was about to happen. This was a new way of thinking about it.

Then I remembered the weird vision I had had at Shady Glen, when my eyes were closed and I saw the view that turned out to be from Rainy Day's stall. Could I possibly have the intuition these authors were talking about? I turned to a random page in the middle of *Open Channels* and read:

> *Communication between humans and animals is not a magic trick. It is not mind-reading. It does, however, require empathy, imagination, and an open heart, which requires a slowing down of thought and feeling. Slowing down our feelings takes a tremendous amount of energy. Think about when you have felt extreme fear. Time seems to slow down, and you notice every tiny sound—a small whine in the distance, a creak in a room upstairs. When the feeling of fear finally passes and you "return to your senses," you may feel exhausted.*

I read those words over and over again and tried to make sense of them. Was it possible that I was more alert to Rainy Day because of my fear? Was it possible to tune in to him through other feelings instead of fear—like love, for instance? Would I eventually be able to communicate with *him*?

After an hour of sitting on the floor reading, I took all four books to the front desk. As I passed through the middle of the library, I noticed a guy in a wheelchair bent over a big rectangular table spread with books and papers. He never looked up.

"You've got quite a pile there," the librarian said with a smile as she scanned the bar code inside the first book. "You can keep them for three weeks. But you can always renew if you're not quite finished."

I loaded the books into my empty backpack and headed home. It was just starting to drizzle when I left the library, but by the time I put my bike away and walked in our door, the rain was coming down hard.

Chase jumped up against my legs.

"Hi, Chase." I patted him on the head and scratched his ears.

Probably because of what I had just been reading, it hit me that in a way, my dog and I talked all the time. Chase said hi by jumping up against my legs. I said hi by saying the word *hi*. I was always telling Chase to do this or that. All those commands I took for granted: *Come! Sit! Eat your dinner! Go outside! Get down off the couch!* I said the words, but Chase was responding to other sources of information— my tone, my gestures, the expression on my face.

"Chase," I said, opening the back door. "Go on outside."

Of course he did, but I knew he did that out of habit, not because I told him to. Chase went straight to the back fence on the other side of the yard, just like he always did. For more drastic communication, I supposed I needed to slow down and experience a stronger feeling. But where Chase was concerned, I didn't seem to have any strong feelings. At least not right then.

I went into the kitchen and pulled open what Aunt Patti and I call "the junk drawer," the place most people kept various tools, pens, rubber bands, and other stuff. For us, it was more like a "junk food drawer," our stash of all the leftover Halloween candy and other salty and sweet stuff that accumulated. Right now it still had a few chocolate hearts and things left over from Valentine's Day months before. I grabbed a miniature box of Hot Rocks and leaned into the drawer to close it.

Tipping a small pile of Hot Rocks into my palm, I tried to muster all the love I could for my dog. I thought about all the time we spent curled up together watching TV, and all the times he greeted me after school when nobody was in the house, and how he used to do whatever Lowell and I asked him to do back when we were little. I popped the cinnamon candies into my mouth, closed my eyes, and concentrated. *Chase*, I thought, *go find your chewed-up stuffed mouse and bring it back into the house. I think it's outside under Aunt Patti's snowball bush.*

The phone ringing broke my concentration. I ran into the living room and found the cordless among the stuff on my bureau. It was Lowell.

"Hey," he said.

"Hi!"

"Where've you been?" he said.

"The library." It didn't sound like this was a good time to tell Lowell about animal communicating. "What are you up to?"

"Nothing." There was a long silence. I turned my face away from the phone and kept eating Hot Rocks, waiting for him to say something more. "You know what, April? Everything sucks."

"You know what, Lowell? Everything does not suck." I didn't bother to keep the frustration from my voice. "A lot may be terrible in your family right now, and I know there are reasons for what's going on, but if you want to get out of your situation, you're going to have to get out of your room. You should come over. Just bring your homework and come over," I demanded. "But make a run for it because it's really pouring."

Just then Aunt Patti walked in the door hello-ing right and left to find me.

"April, hon?"

"I gotta go Lowell. Come over now."

I met up with Aunt Patti by the kitchen door. She slipped out of her poncho and hung it out over the rail on the back porch. She had just turned around when Lowell came bursting through the door.

"Well, hi there, my friend," Aunt Patti said. Then she turned to me. "How are you doing? You must be exhausted. I can't remember you ever getting up as early as you did today. And I don't mean to be bratty, but getting up and out was no mean feat for me, either."

"I feel fantastic!" I replied enthusiastically.

"Good!" she said. "I was afraid you'd be a total wreck."

Lowell and I sat at the tiny kitchen table while Aunt Patti shuffled around making dinner. I told them about the morning with Marty, and what I'd learned at the library. One by one I pulled the books out of my backpack. Lowell flipped through them until Aunt Patti asked him to peel potatoes.

"And you can wash lettuce, April," she added.

"Lowell," I said, "there's going to be a lot to do when Rainy Day gets here. Probably more than I can manage on my own with school and everything. Will you be able to help me out?"

"I don't know," he said in that dead voice of his. "Maybe."

Aunt Patti and I looked at each other.

"Supper's ready. April, feed Chase, will you, please?"

I filled Chase's bowl, called him in, and sat down to eat. After cleaning up dinner, we went into the living room and collapsed on the sofa. By now nobody was home at Lowell's house. His mom was in St. Louis cleaning office buildings, and his dad was parked on a bar stool in St. Clair. Even though he wasn't saying much, I didn't need words to know that Lowell just felt better hanging with us rather than being home alone. It was the same way that Black Beauty understood his trainer John. Black Beauty eventually came to know what John meant even though he didn't comprehend John's words. When I had first read that passage it didn't mean very much to me, but after taking care of the horses that morning and thinking about Lowell, it was beginning to make sense. Sometimes we don't say anything at all and a person can know exactly what we mean. As I had learned that afternoon, there was obviously a big zone of communication that had nothing at all to do with words.

"There's something wet and squeaky behind this pillow," Lowell said, twisting around and digging into the sofa. "What..?"

"Oh, my gosh!" I said. "It's Chase's mouse!"

"Gross," Lowell said.

I looked at Chase, but he was laid out flat on his side and his eyes were shut. There was no telling how long that mushy wet mouse had been there.

Exactly one week later, Aunt Patti left work early so we could go with Marty to pick up Rainy Day at Shady Glen. I sat in the middle of the front seat of Marty's pickup, so excited that my stomach flopped around like a fish at the bottom of a boat. A small horse trailer was hitched to the back of the truck, and I kept looking back to make sure that it was really there. In a little while Rainy Day would be inside it.

All week I had been reading horse books and getting up early to go over to Marty's place. Later in the week I went over after school, too. I did chores, of course, but I also learned the basics about riding. Friendly little Left Bank, who I eventually learned was named for a neighborhood in Paris, was the first horse I mounted. From the moment I stuck my foot in the stirrup and swung up and over into the saddle, I knew I was where I was meant to be. I looked down at Marty and grinned.

"You've just been a rusty old lock," he said. "The pieces all fit together, but so much junk got built up you couldn't make the key work. All we've done is applied a little grease to the works, April."

Evening out the reins in my hand, I laughed. I was growing used to Marty's way of talking. What he said almost always seemed silly, but most of the time the way he put things made me understand better. All the stories I read helped, too. After *Black Beauty*, I knew I could never yank hard on the reins. I remembered poor Ginger, and how she had suffered from harsh training. "Pretend the reins are cobwebs," Marty said. "A horse is more sensitive than you think. He'll know what you want."

Marty taught me the things you could learn about a horse just by watching and listening. I had read about pinned ears meaning the horse was angry or disturbed. But Marty also showed how a relaxed horse will loosen his lower lip. An irritated horse will swish his tail or wrinkle his nose. A snort means the horse might be curious or nervous. The more I learned, the less afraid I felt.

"And always remember how good he can see," Marty said. "The horse has got the biggest eyeball of any land mammal on earth. You ain't gonna hide nothin' from him, so don't even try."

That week, Marty and some of his friends hauled over a prefab mini-barn for our backyard. It had a nice stall, big windows, and room for the tack and feed. When Aunt Patti saw it, she fussed that now she would never be able to put up the greenhouse she had always wanted. But when it was finally placed in a back corner of our property under an old elm tree, even she had to admit that it looked like a cozy place for a horse to live. I couldn't wait until Rainy Day moved in.

Marty and I brought over a load of tack from the storage place where all my parents' supplies had been kept. On the wall I hung the bridles, the halters, the saddle blankets, and the two saddles. I arranged all the grooming tools on the shelves. As a present, Marty gave me buckets and hoses and a big sack of oats. I promised Aunt Patti (who was nervous about this, too) that I would figure out how to earn extra money to pay for feed and supplies so that we wouldn't, as she said, "have to live on rice and spaghetti for the rest of our lives."

On the way to Shady Glen I was too excited to talk. For the first time in days the sun was shining, and I listened to Aunt Patti and Marty discuss the weather. It was the only thing people in Plattsburgh talked about.

"We're about at the supersaturation point," Aunt Patti

said. "There's no place left for this water to go."

"I got a couple friends down in Shannon Fields who've moved out to live with family," Marty said. "They say the creek's higher than anyone's seen it since ninety-three."

"I don't know why that trailer park was developed down there in the first place," Aunt Patti said. "It's always been a disaster waiting to happen."

"Nobody else wants to live there, that's why," Marty explained.

Leigh met us at the door of Shady Glen. Jumping out of the truck, I noticed that it was calmer and quieter than it had been the day after the accident: No longer were there a million people running around with bandages and medical supplies. No one was rushing off to talk on cell phones. It seemed more like the tucked-away refuge it was meant to be, a place where rescued animals could live in peace. The pigs wandered freely in the low grass on the side of the road. I saw a couple of horses making quick playful dashes in the paddock outside the barn.

"Here we are," Aunt Patti announced.

"Welcome back," Leigh said. "Why don't you two come on into my office for a minute? I'd like to have one more chat before we sign all the paperwork."

In the office Leigh looked serious and spoke mostly to

me, making me feel like I was in the principal's office. She explained again that this was a hastier adoption than the Humane Society typically allowed.

"But I've had several conversations with Marty and also your aunt Patti. I've visited the setup you've got, April, and it looks ideal. I just want to make sure you really understand what you're doing here. You will be responsible for Rainy Day for the rest of his life. His life will be literally in your hands." She looked at Aunt Patti and Marty. "In your hands and in the hands of the adults who take care of you."

I took a deep breath. "I understand," I said.

Sometimes I told teachers I understood something when I really didn't, just so I could stop thinking about what they were trying to explain. Maybe later on I would understand, or maybe I wouldn't. But that day at Shady Glen I really and truly *did* understand the importance of what Leigh was saying. I hoped it showed. I guess it did, because Aunt Patti signed the papers and within minutes I was walking over to Rainy Day's stall.

"Hey there, good boy," I murmured, patting him on the nose. He nuzzled my arm. "Today's the day I get to take you home with me."

I slipped into the stall and pulled Rainy Day's blue

halter off the hook. I was especially gentle while putting it on his head, bringing the bands over his face and around the top of his head. Once it was buckled, I stood for a moment and petted him, careful to avoid the place where his stitches had been.

"It's hard to believe we're standing here like this after what we've been through," I whispered, putting one arm across his shoulders and bringing my cheek up against his. "All I know is that if this is happening, anything is possible."

He blew air from his nostrils.

"Be patient with me, though," I said, backing away and attaching the lead rope under his chin. "I'm no expert . . . yet."

I led Rainy Day out to the trailer. His feet clomped up the ramp and we closed the door behind him. I saw a few other horses stick their heads out of the barn windows as we drove away. Part of me felt sad that they would be staying, but I knew that all the Shady Glen people would take good care of them. And as Leigh said, horses are social. They had one another.

We were home by five o'clock. The yard looked pretty, with Aunt Patti's yellow-and-white daffoldils and purple hyacinths lining the driveway. Bees and butterflies were dipping in and out of the blooms, and our big decorative grasses were like green fountains. It had been gray and rainy for a long time, but that afternoon the sunshine made the yard pop with color. Marty whistled.

"This here horse has hit the jackpot," he remarked.

Aunt Patti looked serious. "I'm assuming you guys are planning on setting up a grazing area separate from the garden," she said. "It's hard enough keeping rabbits out of those plots. I can't even imagine what a horse would do to the arugula and parsley."

She put her arm around my shoulder so I knew she was kidding. "For now, though, go ahead and walk him around the whole place. If necessary, you can clean up after him once he's in the barn."

Marty helped me guide Rainy Day out of the trailer before joining Aunt Patti on our back porch.

I led Rainy Day through into the yard. First we walked around the perimeter, clockwise and then counter-clockwise. Then we made a couple of figure eights through the center. A few times Rainy Day wanted to stop and nibble grass or sniff at certain flowers, but I kept him walking, talking to him quietly and reassuring him that this was his new home.

"You'll have loads of time to explore on your own, just not right now," I said, careful to avoid leading him through any of Aunt Patti's well-tended plots. We finished our little tour and stopped by the fence.

I glanced across the gravel driveway into Lowell's yard and was surprised to see him lying facedown in the patchy, muddy grass. I led Rainy Day closer to the fence and realized that Lowell was actually doing push-ups on a panel of plywood laid on the ground. Push-ups?

I watched him until he stopped. Then he got up and went over to the old play set. Lowell reached up to grab the top rail and dangled there for a minute.

"What in the world is he doing, Rainy Day?" I murmured. "I was hoping to introduce you, but he seems to be busy right now."

Lowell tried to lift himself into a chin-up. He made it about a third of the way and then dropped to the ground in a crumpled heap. Then he got up and kicked the swing, sending it flying crookedly on its rusty chain. Lowell must have been deep in his own world not to notice me standing with a horse only twenty yards away. Figuring that was for the best under the circumstances, I led Rainy Day to the back porch, where Aunt Patti and Marty were still sitting, drinking a couple of sodas. We talked about Rainy Day's routine and the best way to handle the rest of that day.

"He'll like the company of your dog," Marty said, smiling. "Most horses do. Dogs, goats, or what have you."

"Good thing school's almost out," Aunt Patti said. "This is going to take up a lot of your time, April."

"She's a kid," Marty laughed. "She got nothing in the world but time."

Rainy Day bent his head down and tore up a mouthful of grass. Aunt Patti inhaled sharply and looked at me.

"I think I'd better show Rainy Day into the barn now," I said to Marty.

We spent the next week establishing a daily routine. Rainy Day took instantly to his mini-barn, and I loved being in there, too. I moved a table and chair into the supply area so that I could do my homework. I also started a logbook in order to keep track of what I needed to remember to do. Marty showed me how to set this up. The log was actually a large green ledger pad. Each page represented one week. Across the top from left to right were seven columns, one for every day of the week. Down the left side were the chores and other things I needed to do for Rainy Day—varieties and amounts of feed, quantities of water, baths, grooming, stall cleaning, medicine (if necessary), training accomplishments, time spent turned out. There was a space at the bottom for me to make additional notes about things that only happened on certain days. That was also where I kept track of anything that seemed interesting and worth remembering, like if he seemed to show happiness at Chase coming to visit, or if he got something unusual to eat. One day he nosed open the sliding lock of his mini-barn door. First I made a note, and then I asked Marty to switch the lock to something Rainy Day wouldn't be able to open. It got so I looked forward to making entries in the log. It also made me less worried that I would forget something important. Marty used the same setup for all the horses stabled at his place.

"Unless you've got a computer for a brain, you need to keep track," he told me, after praising my diligent record-keeping.

"Why don't you just keep track on a computer?" I asked, closing the ledger. "I'm sure there are programs for this kind of thing."

"Call me a backwards caveman, but I'd rather have it all in hard writing. Also, I like it in a book that I can keep in the barn with all the other stuff. No electricity, no battery, no nothing."

The other thing Marty insisted was that I learn all the anatomical parts of the horse from head to tail. To do this, I parked myself in the stall with Rainy Day and opened one of my many books. Some of the words I knew because they were names for human parts, too—hip, leg, back, shoulder, breast, chin, cheek. Other words sounded familiar from the horse stories I had been reading. Poll. Hock. Pastern. Dock. Stifle. Croup. By comparing the labeled picture in the book with Rainy Day, in a short time I knew what every one of these words meant and where they were found. It seemed crazy, but the moment I knew I could tell the withers from the fetlock was the moment I began to think of myself as a horse person. Maybe Marty had known this would happen.

"Marty," I asked on the fifth day after bringing Rainy Day home, "how did you get involved with horses in the first place?"

We were sitting on our back porch after dinner. Lavender shadows gathered across the yard as the sun went down. Rainy Day had already been put to bed for the night.

"I don't ever remember not wanting to be around horses," he said, grinning. "But I wanted to race 'em. I wanted to fly across fields on the back of a horse. Who doesn't? Lucky for me, I was little, and everybody told me I had a future as a jockey. I was in Tennessee growing up, and that's what people like me did. My daddy took me down to Florida. He got a job and set me up with a trainer there."

As it grew dark, the fireflies floated around the yard, switching on and off. Marty had fallen silent, but it didn't seem like that was the end of his story.

"Did you like being a jockey?" I asked, hoping he would go on.

"I loved it more than anything I'd ever done," he said quickly. "One spring during a morning workout I was riding a two-year-old. A horse full of heart. Loved nothing more than running as fast as he could, which suited me just fine. Moonshine, he was called. That morning, as a special treat, I gave him his head completely. Which means I loosened up on the reins and let him take the track as fast as he wanted. We were partners and I trusted him to know best. But Moonshine tripped in the straightaway and fell. Compound fracture and had to be put down. All in less time than it takes you to tie your shoe. I just couldn't race any more after that. Came up here to Missouri because there were other kinds of horse work to be had."

We sat silent in the gathering darkness. Just then I heard steps in the yard next door. It was Lowell walking out by the play set. I could only see his silhouette, but I was able to watch his dark, bulky shape reach up and dangle from the top rail. Slowly and steadily, Lowell hoisted his chin to the rail four times in a row.

Even though I wanted to, I knew better than to call out and applaud.

chapter

One Saturday morning about a week later, Marty pushed me and Rainy Day out of our routine. I was perfectly happy hanging around our yard and the ring at Marty's place, but Marty had said that Rainy Day had proven himself to be a steady and reliable horse. Now it was time for us to get out on our own and try something new. I had my doubts, but I also had enough faith in Marty's judgment to go along with the plan. Chase followed me to the back door as if he intended to come, too.

"You stay here, Chase. Today we're going a little farther than you're used to."

Once he was saddled, Rainy Day seemed surprised and reluctant to be led toward the gate of our yard.

"It's okay," I said, turning around and rubbing his face. I avoided touching the pinkish, almost healed scar from the accident. "It's time for a change of scenery."

I mounted into the saddle and rode Rainy Day at a slow walk through town. After two or three days of sunshine, the clouds and rain had returned. The shoulders of the smaller streets in town were muddy, and you could see large standing puddles surrounding the fast-food chains on Route 50. On the outskirts of town, the parking lot of the big outlet stores was a lake. Even the tiny creeks, the ones that were dry most of the year, had swollen into mini-rivers. Rainy Day's hooves clomped and sloshed through the brownish slop.

Two miles north of town, we turned off Route 50 onto Boone's Passage. I held Rainy Day to the middle of the old dirt road where the gravel was mounded a little higher.

"You don't want to be walking in that ooze," I said. "Let's get moving a little faster."

I clucked my tongue, loosened the reins, and squeezed my knees into his sides. Rainy Day shook his head and quickened his pace into a gentle trot.

I was happy to be outside of town. The trees were in full leaf and, along both sides of the road, wildflowers bloomed in a rainbow of colors. Tiny yellow, purple, blue, pink, and white blossoms looked like dabs of paint on top of long fragile stems. Dragonflies, butterflies, and hummingbirds gathered nectar busily. Even though the sky was slate gray, the temperature was perfect. May can be boiling in Missouri, but that morning it seemed to be a perfect seventy degrees.

Pretty soon, to my own surprise, I felt an impulse to go faster than a trot. I'd wanted to try a canter during lessons, too, but Marty hadn't let me. He had made me promise not to try new paces when he wasn't around. Still, I thought about giving Rainy Day just a small nudge to take us into a canter. I was just about to do so when something made me stop. A feeling came over me that made me sense the word *no*. It was like a rush of wind that pushed me away from doing what I had planned. The moment came and went in a flash, but I felt that the message had come from Rainy Day. "I get it," I said, patting his neck.

I forced myself to be patient and we continued down the road. It was a nice feeling, that steady two-beat rocking motion of the walk—clip-*clop*, clip-*clop*, clip-*clop*, clip-*clop*. Moving at that lazy, rhythmic pace, I felt almost hypnotized.

A black turkey vulture in the road up ahead snapped me out of my daze. When he saw us approaching, he took one last peck at a run-over squirrel and flew off. Just past where the vulture had been, I saw a break in the woods on the right-hand side of the road. Set back in a large overgrown yard was a ramshackle old farmhouse. An American flag hung from a pole planted near the roadside next to a black mailbox. Both the mailbox and the flagpole stood at odd angles to the ground, as if they had been knocked off center by a charging bull. As we approached, an old man walked out to put a letter in the mailbox. "Morning," the man said, looking up at me as I was about to pass.

"Whoa," I said quietly. Rainy Day halted.

"Good morning," I said.

"You're up early," he said. "New in town?"

"No. I've just never been out this way before."

You always read stories about old men who have a twinkle in their eye. This one, I had to admit, didn't have any twinkle in either of his eyes. He just stared at me in a grouchy kind of way. I looked down, wondering if I should move on or stay and chat. Purple and yellow irises were growing around the base of the mailbox. I recognized the bulbs because they were Aunt Patti's favorite. "Each one takes a different shape," she would say. "They're not cookie-cutter blooms like tulips or daffodils." Here they were mixed in with the kinds of tall weeds that drove Aunt Patti crazy in our backyard—goldenrod, thistle, stinging nettle, and clover. Someone had obviously stopped weeding this little iris patch.

The old man passed very close to Rainy Day's face and started to open the front of his mailbox. The hinges were so rusty, the door wouldn't budge.

"Darn this rain and darn this thing."

He clamped his letter between his lips and used both hands to shake the whole tippy mailbox on its unsturdy stand.

"Maybe I can help," I said. I dismounted and pulled the reins over Rainy Day's head, tying them in a loose knot to the fence rail.

Getting the little mailbox door open wasn't difficult. I put one leg on the base, one hand on the main section of the box, and yanked sharply on the hook that was mounted to the door. The old man stuck in his letter and I shut the door. He raised the red flag on the side of the box.

"Atta girl," he said, smiling for the first time. His teeth were long, yellow, and stained in places from tobacco.

I smiled back. "No problem."

"You are who?" he said.

"April Helmbach."

"From Plattsburgh?"

Behind his pale gray eyes, I could see the old man's mind racing along making connections.

"Joseph McCann," he said. "Been here forever. Your father went to school with my kids here in town. Your aunt did the flowers for my wife's funeral a couple of years ago. Nice job she did."

He stuck out his hand and we shook. Then he reached out to pat Rainy Day, who was watching us the whole time.

"And this is?" he asked, raising his bushy eyebrows.

"Rainy Day."

"Good boy," Mr. McCann said. "How'd you get that scar, old man?"

"He was in that accident on Fifty-four earlier this month," I explained. "He's just about healed, though," I said, rubbing his flank. Under my hand, his skin was twitching at the black flies that landed on him the minute he stopped moving.

"See that gal?" Mr. McCann pointed past the house to a fenced paddock. A large bay horse grazed in the grass and swished at flies with her tail. "That's Hannah. Quarter horse going on fifteen. She's with foal and getting pretty darn uncomfortable now that it's getting hotter. I bet she'd love the company, if you ever feel like bringing Rainy Day over to visit. She belongs to my daughter, but my daughter moved up to Chicago so it's just me here taking care of everyone."

"Everyone?"

"Oh, everyone. I got a couple of everything around here. I got goats, I got hens, I got a pig, and I got geese. My name oughta be Noah insteada McCann. You can't see the barn from here. It's down aways closer to the creek."

"You run this place all by yourself?"

"More or less. One by one our kids up 'n' left. They tell me Plattsburgh's, well, Plattsburgh."

"What do they mean by that?" I asked.

"They mean it's the kind of place that just stays the same no matter what. And then I tell *them* that a place can't change if the young people don't stay and *make* it change."

I didn't know what to say, but Rainy Day stomped a hoof. Then Mr. McCann's quarter horse lifted her head and turned to face us. She nickered. Rainy Day nickered back.

"I can come back some other time," I offered, feeling sorry all of a sudden for this lonely old man. "I've got a couple more weeks of school but then I'm done. I do need to find a summer job to help pay for Rainy Day's supplies. But maybe I could visit when I get a chance. It's a real nice ride out here."

I untied and mounted Rainy Day.

"Don't be a stranger," Mr. McCann called out as we turned to head back to town.

When I got home, Marty was sitting in his truck at the end of our driveway. He folded up the newspaper as Rainy Day and I walked slowly toward the barn.

"It's messy as heck out there, April," he said, climbing out of the driver's seat. "I thought I'd stop by to make sure you know what you're doing cleaning Rainy Day up from a ride like that. How'd it go?"

"It was a blast," I said, swinging out of the saddle and leading Rainy Day to the hitching rail. First I unbuckled the girth. Then I removed the saddle and carried it into the shed. I took off the saddle pad and draped it over its rack. Finally I pulled off his bridle and put on his halter. I carried out the bin with all the grooming supplies and put it down in front of Rainy Day. While patting his face, I inspected him all over. His legs were especially splashed and encrusted with mud.

"You're filthy," I said. "This is going to take a while, and I'm starving."

Marty laughed. "But just think how good that breakfast will taste when you're done."

I began with the currycomb, making gentle circles to get out all the dirt. I started to move down one of his legs, but Rainy Day turned his head to look at me disapprovingly.

"Don't curry the legs down there," Marty said. "They're too sensitive and he won't like it. You'll have to use a sponge and a brush."

"I don't know if I can get the socks clean that way. You can hardly see that he's got white socks, he's so dirty."

"Well, you have to try," Marty said firmly.

After sponging his legs, I began to pick out the hooves. Even though I trusted Rainy Day completely and had been grooming him for a few weeks, holding his foot in my hand still made me a little nervous. Especially that morning, when the gunk and mud on the bottom of his feet were sticky and dark. It took all my concentration to flick out the little stones lodged under his hooves.

"I know it's a lot," Marty said. "But you're doing great. And you have no choice. A horse is nothing without his feet. No feet, no horse."

It was getting hotter now, and I knew Rainy Day would like it if I ran the hose over him. I soaped him up, conditioned his tail and mane, and rinsed him off. Then I brushed him until his coat, tail, and mane were shiny and smooth. When I led him back into his stall for a big tub of oats, he looked like one of the gleaming show horses I read about in *Blue Grass Rider* magazine.

"Enjoy," I said. "I'll see you later. Thanks for a great ride." Rainy Day leaned into the tub for a mouthful of oats and started munching happily.

I had completely forgotten about Marty and jumped when he spoke.

"Nicely done," he said approvingly.

"Thanks." I said it calmly, but inside I was beaming.

"So tell me about the ride. Any surprises outside the ring? Usually there are."

We walked over to the back porch and sat down.

"Well, I met this old guy out on Boone's Passage. He has a working farm, with animals and all, including an old quarter horse. It looked like a nice place but it was also a little sad because I guess his wife died and all his kids have moved away. He said he knew my parents."

Marty nodded.

"Old Joe McCann," he said. "A good farmer and a good man. And ...?"

"And we just talked a little while. Then we headed home. Kind of a weird thing happened, though."

"Weird how?" Marty asked.

"We were trotting, and it was so nice out and the pace felt so comfortable. I felt like it would be fine to move into the canter. But then something told me not to. It was like a hunch. A feeling in the pit of my stomach. So of course I didn't do it. What was that all about, do you think?"

Marty paused before answering.

"Hard to say right now. What do *you* think?"

I wasn't quite ready to say aloud what I really thought, namely that Rainy Day had communicated with me through intuition. And then another thought popped into my head.

"Marty? Remember the other day, when I cantered in the ring by accident?"

"April, that wasn't no accident. That happened because you didn't convey to Rainy Day *not* to transition into the canter. You let him tell *you* what to do in the ring that day, which can't ever happen with a horse."

Marty had never sounded so forceful. "You have to be the boss," he continued. "Always. Think of it this way—a horse wants you to be the boss. He may even do what he can to *help* you be the boss."

"How so?" I didn't understand what a horse could do to get *me* to lead *him*.

"If you're paying attention, you might pick up on Rainy

Day's fear about doing something. Then you'll know not to try it just then."

So maybe Rainy Day had felt okay about cantering in the ring, but had not been quite ready to canter with me out on the open road. Maybe I *had* picked up on his feelings, as I suspected. Everything Marty was saying began to make sense.

"A gelding is happiest in the herd," Marty finally concluded. "Being one of the guys. You, my friend, have to be happiest as his herd leader."

It was still hard to imagine myself as a leader. I dangled my legs off the porch and used a stick to get some of the mud off the bottom of my boots.

"You've come a long way, I don't deny that," Marty said. "But I need to see you really master the slower gaits before you take things up a notch. The basic action of the horse is the most important thing to understand."

"What do you mean action?" I asked.

"I mean, the way he collects himself, all the parts of his body from front to back and top to bottom. Getting it all under control and coordinated, all wound up and ready to go. Every gait must be collected and in control."

Suddenly Marty leaned sharply into my side. I nearly fell over.

"See?" he said.

"See what?"

"See how you lost your balance for a second there when I pushed you?" Marty asked. "You bounced right back up again without even realizing it. Just a natural reaction, right?"

"Um, yeah, I guess so."

"This is what I'm talking about. All the action of a horse at any gait is about the loss of balance and the recovery of balance. The way you handle him can help him establish good balance and form. Do this perfectly while walking and trotting and then we can talk about cantering."

"And galloping?" I asked.

Marty gave me another sharp shove so that I tipped over for real.

"When the time comes," he said with a smile, clapping me on the shoulder as I sat back up.

Behind us, the screen door opened with a squeak.

"I thought I heard voices," Aunt Patti said. "Hi, Marty. You two ready for some lunch?"

"Lunch?" I said. "How about breakfast?"

Aunt Patti laughed. "It's nearly noon, but I guess I could scramble us some eggs. Your new life as an early bird is going to take some adjusting."

Aunt Patti stepped down from the porch onto the grass. "Ugh. Look at this place. The hostas are happy, the hydrangeas are happy, and the mint, as always, is happy. But my poor mums—they need to dry out pretty soon or else. How long can this keep up? I never expected Plattsburgh to turn into a rain forest. Maybe I ought to be growing orchids and banana trees."

Over lunch we talked about Mr. McCann. Aunt Patti remembered him well. She said he had a nice family. One of his younger sons had been in her class in elementary school.

"I felt bad for the whole family when she died," Aunt Patti said. "I think it was one of those situations where the mom held everything together—kept up with the kids even when they were grown, took care of Mr. McCann and the house. At her funeral, which must have been about two or three years ago, they all looked totally stricken."

"Well," I said, buttering my toast, "at least the flowers made him happy."

"I'm glad about that," Aunt Patti said. "I tried really hard to get it right. Everyone told me Mrs. McCann loved irises, just like me, so I put them everywhere, in all different colors."

Aunt Patti stopped and thought, remembering that day.

"For a while I wondered how he'd get along on his own," she said finally. "You know, I think it'd be great for you to visit him, if you're passing that way again."

After lunch Marty left and I rode my bike to the library. I wanted to return the books I had borrowed and check out some new ones. It felt odd riding a bicycle after spending the morning on horseback—nothing to think about but pushing pedals and steering.

I put all the books on the counter and went straight back to the animal section. My English teacher had recommended a book called *All Creatures Great and Small*, about a veterinarian in England. She said there were great stories about all kinds of animals, including horses.

On my way to the stacks I heard a cough. I looked over at one of the tables and saw the same guy in a wheelchair who was there before. Just like the other day, he had a pile of books spread in front of him. It was hard to tell his age, but I guessed he was around twenty-two. He wore a tight camo-patterned T-shirt, and had very strong-looking arms. He had a clipped goatee and mustache, and the hair on his head was really short.

The librarian went over to him.

"Shawn, I think I've found the site you were wondering about. Come over here to the computer and I can show you." She walked away toward the front desk.

"Great," he said, pushing away from the table and zooming backward.

He followed the librarian, giving the big rear wheels of his chair two or three energetic pumps. The chair was small and sleek, not like those huge unwieldy ones you see being pushed around in hospitals. I noticed that his legs seemed very skinny, especially compared to his upper body. I tried not to stare, but it was hard not to look.

I went over to the animal stacks and tried to mind my own business. I found the book my teacher had mentioned and pulled it off the shelf, along with an oversize book about the horse's digestive system. Marty had told me to be on the lookout for feeding problems because they were "the number one thing that goes wrong with a horse." Anyhow, I was worried about getting Rainy Day's feed just right. I also couldn't resist pulling out an old-looking hardback with yellowed pages. When I opened it, I noticed that musty, damp-old-library-book smell. I liked the book's black-and-white photographs of real kids doing things with their horses—bathing, grooming, leading, riding, and brushing. When I finally headed back to the front desk, I had six or seven books balanced uncomfortably in my arms.

By now the guy in the wheelchair was back at his table working. As I passed I accidentally dropped *All Creatures Great and Small*. Before I could bend over to pick it up, the guy flicked his arm down like a snake and scooped it up for me.

"Here you go," he said.

"Thanks."

"That's what happens when you try to carry more than you can hold," he said.

"I guess so."

"My name's Shawn. Shawn Clarke." He smiled.

"I'm April."

"I roll around on wheels. I see you walk on legs," he said jokingly.

"Yeah, I started doing this around twelve years ago." I laughed.

He laughed, too, and stuck out his hand. I put my books down on the table so we could shake.

"Touché," he said. "Some people think it's better to pretend they don't see that I can't walk, so I've gotten in the habit of breaking the ice that way. You're the first person to nail me right back." He nodded to my books. "What are you reading about?"

"Horses," I said, relieved the awkwardness was gone.

This guy looked kind of tough, but his eyes were bright blue and shining like an excited kid's. I sat down at the desk. "What about you?" I glanced at all the books on the table.

"I know I look a little old to be in school," Shawn said, "but I'm studying for the college entrance tests. It's late to be applying to college, but I've got my reasons."

Shawn explained that right after high school he had enlisted in the army.

"I had no wife, no kids, a high school diploma, and an okay but dead-end job at a bakery here in town. I figured it was the right thing to do, to serve our country and all. That's how I was raised."

"So where did you end up?"

"Iraq."

"Whoa," I said. "How long were you there?" I didn't know too much about the war, but from here and there I had picked up that it was a pretty intense situation.

"Just over two years," Shawn said. "I got promoted to army specialist. Specialist Clarke."

"Oh, well, that's good, right? I mean, getting promoted?"

"It just meant that I had men under me."

Shawn sneered but I had no idea why.

"Sorry," he said, "but that word still gets me. From the beginning we were always called men. When I was promoted I was nineteen! Way closer to a boy than a man. At least I felt that way at the time. But being promoted meant I was responsible for kids younger than me, which kind of changes how you look at things. It changes what you're willing to do. What you expect of yourself."

Shawn seemed to get lost in thought and I didn't know what to say. Eventually he went on.

"A lot of things happened I won't go into. Anyway, last fall, when we were riding out to patrol a small village outside of Baghdad, our vehicle ran over a roadside bomb. Some of us got hurt, a few pretty badly. Compared to the others, I was lucky. So here I am back in Plattsburgh."

As we were talking, the librarian approached with another reference book for Shawn. She seemed to know him pretty well.

"Shawn," the librarian asked, "I meant to ask: Are you and your mom still down on Christina Street?"

"We are. Same street, same trailer," he confirmed.

"And how is she?"

"Okay, thanks. Mom's down visiting her sister in Little Rock for a few weeks but she'll be back in July."

"Maybe that's good," the librarian said. "No distractions

from studying for the ACT and SATs, right?"

"What's that?" I asked.

"Those tests I told you about," Shawn said. "I'm not going to be good for much at all if I don't get my brain trained. The way I see it, it's use it or lose it. My dad served in Vietnam, and his dad fought in World War II. I don't know if that's why, but both my dad and grandpa said the world would always need people who could think for themselves."

The librarian agreed.

"April," she said, "I thought I'd better mention that it's looking like rain again and you're on your bike. I love your company here, but I think you probably ought to get going."

I got my books scanned, loaded them into my backpack, and went out to unlock my bike. Shawn rolled out through the glass door behind me. A battered green army duffel was slung onto one handle of his wheelchair as he drove the wheels forward with his strong arms.

"Hey, April. Nice to meet you."

"Yeah, nice to meet you, too."

"One day you'll have to tell me all about horses."

"I will," I said, and pedaled off.

On the way home I wondered whether Shawn really

meant it when he asked about horses. Something about his story had made me think about all the horses in *Black Beauty* and the hard jobs they had to do. Some pulled cabs all night long. Some hauled coal or plowed fields. Others were driven to hunt down rabbits or foxes. And some carried soldiers into battle, participating in wars they never would understand. I understood that these were horse jobs. Still, it seemed incredibly wrong to make horses do work that only ruined them in the end. And I wasn't exactly sure, but I got the feeling that what Shawn had experienced was not all that different—only Shawn wasn't about to let it ruin him.

"Miz Patti," Lowell said. "How long are you going to keep on doing these crazy scrapbooks?"

We were sitting on the couch that Saturday night after dinner. It was raining, of course, but tonight the water was coming down in big fat drops rather than sheets. You know how everyone learns that the Inuit people in Alaska have dozens of words for snow? Teachers explain that this is because snow is something the Inuit live with all the time, so they need precise ways to distinguish among icy snow, soft snow, packed snow, slushy snow, and so on. Here in Plattsburgh, I was beginning to think we needed more words to describe the rain. *Sheets* and *buckets* no longer did the trick. And "raining cats and dogs" was cliché, as my English teacher would say.

"Lowell," Aunt Patti said, her eyes shining playfully, "I'll thank you not to call my hobby crazy. And to answer your question, I'll do this as long as I feel like doing it. It so happens that mimesis is a fascinating subject. Come sit here for a second and I'll show you what I'm talking about."

Lowell groaned, playing along with the old routine he once had with Aunt Patti—bored kid to her cute and enthusiastic nerd. He stood up and went over to sit next to her. I could see that he was starting to look better. His cheeks looked rosy, his skin was clearer, and he moved with more energy in his step. Whenever I looked out back, I saw him doing some kind of exercise—chin-ups or push-ups. Some afternoons I actually saw him jogging home from school. One day after P.E. I noticed him talking to the cross-country coach. And instead of sitting alone in his room tonight, he was hanging out with Aunt Patti and me. I hoped the change would last.

Aunt Patti carefully smoothed down the picture she had last glued into place. From where I sat, it looked like a moth.

"This guy," she said to Lowell, resting a finger on the picture, "appears to its predators to be inedible. His wings look like toxic moldy dead leaves. What bird would want to eat that?" She flipped the page. "And check this out. What's this look like to you, Lowell?"

Lowell stared at the album on the coffee table.

"A pile of sticks."

"It's called a walking stick, but it's actually an insect. Look closer," she instructed, and Lowell leaned in. "It's a bug. But it takes very close observation to see that it's not a couple of dead stalks."

"But eventually the bird is going to figure out it's alive and eat it, right?" Lowell commented.

"Probably," Aunt Patti conceded. "But only after it's had enough time to reproduce. That's all it needs time to do."

It had been a long day and I was tired. I looked at Chase stretched out on the floor like a rug. He was completely relaxed and content, and I realized I felt the same. The only thing I would change to make things better would be a little sunshine the next day. Even an hour's worth. I slid down to the floor and scratched Chase on the stomach. He thumped his tail in gratitude.

Lowell flipped on the television with the remote. He surfed a dozen channels, including all the music video ones that drove Aunt Patti crazy.

"Go to sixty-three," she said.

Lowell and I moaned when we realized it was the weather center. There was the big blanket of gray stretching across the Midwest, as there had been for most of the month. The local reporter announced that parts of Missouri, Iowa, and Illinois were setting record levels of rainfall. The reporter also mentioned that certain low-lying towns along the Meramec and the Bourbeuse Rivers were starting to flood.

"Those places aren't too far from here," Aunt Patti said, putting down her materials, concerned. She took the remote from Lowell and raised the volume. The reporter gave more details while pointing to a huge map of our region.

"Our correspondents in St. Clair and other towns are reporting that several homes and businesses have been evacuated. Many area residents are already making insurance claims on damaged property. Furthermore, because they expect weather conditions to worsen before this immense front makes its way east, local road crews and emergency service providers are preparing for massive operations in the coming days."

I knew things were getting serious when Aunt Patti let us change the channel without making a comment.

A little while later, after settling down to watch sitcom reruns, we heard a car pull up in the driveway between our houses. Lowell got up and looked out the front window. "It's my mom," he said. "I'll take off. Thanks for dinner, Miz Patti. See you, April." He left with a wave.

"Does it seem to you that Lowell is opening up some?" Aunt Patti asked when we were alone.

"I guess so." I shrugged. I felt uncomfortable talking about Lowell with Aunt Patti. It was an unspoken rule that he and I always kept each other's secrets.

"Well, I think it's a good thing. His mom sees a difference, too. She says she's trying to get his dad to notice and try to get closer to him. Lowell's such a smart kid. It's been a shame to see him all shut in and miserable."

I nodded in vague agreement.

There was a lot on my mind when I went off to bed. True, Lowell seemed better and that was great, but I still needed to find a summer job. And I couldn't get Shawn out of my thoughts. He had been so far away from home and everything familiar, and must have seen such scary things. It would take true strength to come back and be with people like me, who couldn't imagine what a real war was like. In some ways he seemed much older than twenty. And of course, there was lonely Mr. McCann. Before finally drifting off to sleep, I decided to go back and visit him next week.

In the middle of the night I woke up to a loud crack of thunder. A minute went by before my room lit up in a ghostly white flash of lightning, and then there was another clap and roll of thunder. Normally I never got scared of storms, but that night I was literally shaking in my sheets.

Terror seeped from my heart into every part of my body.

"Rainy Day?" I said aloud.

It occurred to me without a doubt that the reason I felt so scared was because Rainy Day was terrified. Sitting up in bed, I knew I needed to get out to the barn to be with him. I reached over and switched on my lamp. Then I got out of bed and quickly put on a pair of sweatpants and a sweatshirt. I hurried down the hall and went into the kitchen. Next to the kitchen door I slipped into my yard shoes. As quietly as possible I turned the dead bolt on the door. Although Aunt Patti was a sound sleeper, noise from the storm might have woken her, too, and I didn't want her to tell me to stay put in the house. I pulled a flashlight from our tool drawer and plucked my poncho off its hook. Then I pushed open the screen door and made a mad dash across the yard toward the shed.

Right away I heard Rainy Day stomping his hooves in his box and kicking softly at the wood. He snorted when he heard me come in.

"I'm here now," I said reassuringly. "It's okay, boy. It's okay, Rainy Day." He met me at the opening to his stall and I patted his face, nose, and head. Pointing the flashlight down to the ground so it wouldn't spook him, I turned it on. "I know you're scared, but I'm right here. There's nothing to be scared of. It's just a storm."

Rain seeped through my poncho and I started to shiver. I figured I'd stay another few minutes and then head back to bed. When I turned to leave, Rainy Day let out a loud whinny.

"What? What is it?"

He whinnied again. I knew then that he didn't want me to leave. I patted him some more and whispered comforting messages. Like me, he had started to shiver. I got inside his stall and covered him with a blanket. Then Rainy Day backed away and gave me some space. Before sitting down in the clean hay, I grabbed a second blanket for myself. I leaned back against the stall door and let myself relax. Warming up, I started to drift off to sleep. If Rainy Day didn't want to be alone, I thought, I might as well keep him company. I turned off the flashlight and closed my eyes.

My mind must have been somewhere between asleep and awake, because I started to sense a series of hazy images. First I heard the shriek of tires, and then the crash of crumpling metal. In the darkness of my dream, I sensed horses lying on their sides in a dim light and kicking air silently, trying to get back on their feet. Where was this? It seemed to be a small place of some sort, and the horses were jammed all close together. I understood that I was seeing the accident, imagining it from a different perspective. It was as if I was seeing what Rainy Day had seen right after the crash. In the vision I heard one horse breathing heavily through his nostrils and then suddenly no sound at all. Another horse was trying to breathe, but he was buried under two dead mares. Another horse lay very still, her heart beating faintly. And there was the Thoroughbred, wedged against the side of the truck.

Apart from what I had witnessed that day, I had read accounts of the accident in the newspaper, and Leigh had told me many details about what the animals had experienced. All of these stories seemed to be playing out in my dream.

I felt a nudge on my toes and opened my eyes. Rainy Day had dipped his head low to nose my foot. He shook out his mane and then took a few small steps closer to me.

Could Rainy Day possibly know what I had just seen?

Rainy Day stayed near me for a long time, his nose practically in my lap. I held his whole head and massaged the area around his jaws and chin. I scratched the diamond-shaped patch on his forehead. Then I blew soft puffs of air into each of his nostrils. I had read in a book that one of the ways desert people used to calm their Arabian stallions was to blow in their nostrils. I had no idea whether it would work, but Rainy Day seemed to like it.

By now the storm had passed and the rain had slowed to a drizzle. It was toasty warm and cozy in the barn, but I knew I should go back in the house before Aunt Patti realized I was missing.

"See ya later, boy," I said quietly. I was glad to see Rainy Day close his eyes as I turned to leave.

It felt like I had no sooner put my head down to sleep when I started to dream again. This time I dreamed that Mr. McCann was hammering a sign up on our house. Shawn was sitting in his wheelchair holding the sign in place with his hands and they were laughing together. The sign said

HELP WANTED, and I remember wondering why Mr. McCann and Shawn Clarke would be putting a HELP WANTED sign on our door. The hammering sound continued and I realized that I was no longer dreaming. Someone was actually banging on our front door.

"April," Aunt Patti called in a sleepy voice from her room. "See who it is before you open the door."

It was barely light out, which in late May meant that it was no later than five o'clock in the morning. Getting up on a Sunday morning before ten should be against the law, I thought, as I shuffled into the living room and opened the door.

"Lowell!" I was too surprised and tired to say anything else.

"April, you've got to get up. Things are really crazy out here. The water's high everywhere and it keeps rising. You know Mrs. Baumsdorf on our other side? Well, her cat never came in last night and this morning she went out to see where it was. She walked all the way over to Cumberland Park. On the way, everything was completely soaked, and she said all the grass in the whole park was under a couple of inches of water. It was like that all the way to the lumberyard. Anyway, she heard Lady Jane crying and saw her up in a tree, too afraid to come down because of the water. My mom told me to come get you to see if we could help."

By now I was wide awake. "Should we ask Aunt Patti to drive us over?"

"April, you're not getting it," Lowell said. "The water's really, really high. No car can get anywhere near there. Mrs. Baumsdorf only saw Lady Jane from far away. The water is like up to here." He pointed to his hip. I must have looked as though I didn't believe him. "April, I'm dead serious. This is no joke."

"Come on, then," I said, changing into my boots.

I scrawled a hasty note to Aunt Patti and left it on the counter next to the coffee maker. Then we went out to the barn.

"Long time no see," I said to Rainy Day, patting him on the neck. "Rough night." He snorted and shook his head.

Bridled and saddled, Rainy Day stood still while I adjusted the stirrups.

"We'll eat after this," I promised him. "More oats than you'll know what to do with." I led him out the barn door into the soggy grass of the yard where Lowell was waiting.

"I'm pretty sure he can carry both of us," I said to Lowell. "It's only a short ride. Here. Get on."

Lowell climbed up behind me and we started off. I

couldn't believe my eyes. Our area of Plattsburgh was threaded by tiny creeks, some dry and some running, depending on the time of year. Now it was impossible to tell what was creek and what was land. The whole neighborhood seemed to rise out of a shallow lake. Rainy Day stepped along patiently in water up to his knees and hocks.

A few blocks away, Cumberland Park was entirely submerged. I brought Rainy Day to a halt and tried to get my bearings by looking at the playground. There was no sign of the splintered seesaw or the hard metal carousel. I could only see the very top rail of the swing set. A few yards away grew the oldest elm in town, which everyone had climbed at least once in their life. There, up on a high limb, we saw Mrs. Baumsdorf's gray Persian cat, Lady Jane. She was meowing like crazy for help.

"There she is." I pointed so that Lowell could see. He was leaning back with his two hands propped on Rainy Day's back end. I think he was avoiding putting his arms around my waist, and I was glad. That would have been too awkward even for us.

I clucked Rainy Day forward into the deeper water closer to the elm. He sloshed through the grassy, muddy water without any objection at all. Now the swirling water was up to the main part of his body but at least we were right against the trunk.

"Whoa, Rainy Day! Whoa, boy."

We stopped and looked up into the branches. Lady Jane looked down at us and meowed. Her voice was raspy, probably from having been crying all night.

"Now what?" Lowell said.

I twisted around to face him as best I could. "Now you climb up there and bring her down and we get out of here."

"You're joking, I assume," he said with a straight face.

"Of course I'm not joking. There's nothing else we *can* do."

I held Rainy Day steady, murmuring quietly to keep him comforted. Lowell carefully stood up behind me, planting his feet on Rainy Day's croup, the solid, muscular part between the saddle and the tail.

"Try to get ahold of that lowest branch and pull yourself up. You can wedge your toes into the bark cracks, you know," I said.

"I know, I know."

I watched as Lowell managed to climb higher and higher toward Lady Jane. Obviously, the exercises he had been doing all month were paying off. Thank goodness for those chin-ups.

Lowell came down a little less easily than he had gone

up. He cradled Lady Jane in his left arm and hung on to the tree with the other. That last step down onto Rainy Day was rough. To keep his balance, Rainy Day had to take two sloshing steps forward.

"Jeez, April!" Lowell shouted. "Hang on!"

"Sorry," I said, steadying Rainy Day.

Lady Jane continued to howl. I could feel her pressed against the small of my back. Even though my legs didn't reach all the way down Rainy Day's sides, water was lapping at the bottom of my boots. If it got any deeper, Rainy Day might have to swim, and I wasn't sure if I could ride him that way.

Rainy Day pushed through the deepest part of the water out of the park and towards the road.

"Check out the wooden creek bridge," Lowell said, tapping my shoulder with his free hand and pointing about fifty yards to one side.

"Where?" I asked, looking around.

"That's what I mean. It's gone. It's underwater."

All around us, Plattsburgh appeared to be sinking into a spreading sea. In the east, the sun climbed up over the horizon and shone straight at us. For a second, squeezing my eyes closed against the intense morning light, I couldn't see anything at all.

chapter

It was too wet in Mrs. Baumsdorf's front yard for us to dismount. I rode right up to the edge of her porch and Lowell reached over and passed her Lady Jane. Mrs. Baumsdorf was so relieved and happy, she snuggled her cat under her chin and started to cry. Lady Jane looked like a dirty wet string mop with blue eyes—droopy and exhausted.

I knew Rainy Day would be completely spent after carrying two people, so as soon as we were on more solid ground I told Lowell to get down. He said bye and went into his house. I dismounted then, too, and led Rainy Day into his stall. I gave him a good grooming, fresh water, and several scoops of oats mixed with chunks of carrots and apples.

"How's that for a feast?" I asked. He replied by immediately sticking his nose in his feed bucket and beginning to crunch. I smiled and patted his neck. "Thank you for getting us through that. You deserve more than a bunch of oats, I know, but for now it's all I've got."

Inside the house, Aunt Patti was sitting on the couch,

talking on the phone and watching the weather on mute. I had no idea who she was talking to, but I was so hungry, I didn't care. I went straight to the kitchen to find something to eat. Chase trotted beside me and lay down under the table. I was surprised to see on the oven clock that it was only 7:23. It felt like noon. I put a bagel in the toaster and poured myself a bowl of cold cereal. While I waited for the bagel to brown, I drank a huge glass of orange juice and opened a mini box of raisins, the kind Aunt Patti used to put in my lunch box when I was little. Then I took everything to the table and sat down to eat. I was spreading strawberry jelly on my bagel when Aunt Patti came in. She leaned down and gave me a hug from behind and kissed the top of my head. She was still in her nightgown, her hair was a mess, and the skin of her cheeks was creased from sleep. Normally Aunt Patti looked younger than all my friends' moms, but now she looked practically like a big sister.

"Thanks for the note," she said. "I would have really worried. And the phone's been ringing off the hook," she said. "First Fran, who told me what you and Lowell were doing. She said Lowell came back feeling terrific, like he'd just climbed Mount Everest. Then Mrs. Baumsdorf, who said you and Lowell will be her champions forever."

She paused and watched me chew.

"What's it like out there?" she asked.

"Kinda wet," I said jokingly, and Aunt Patti swiped at my hand gently.

"Actually, it's pretty intense," I said. "I've never seen so much water in places where you're not supposed to see water."

Aunt Patti nodded. She put on her glasses and glanced out the window. I decided not to mention how Lowell looked climbing down a slippery elm tree with a wet cat in one arm, or how deep the water got on the way back.

"That's pretty much what they're saying on the news."

"What do you mean?" I said.

"Well, people are saying this may be it."

"What do you mean—it?"

"I just mean that we may have to find a higher and drier place to stay for a while until this water goes down. We're in the middle of a flash flood, and it may be only the first round. If things get much worse, we can't be here. It's not safe," she said, seeming to will her voice steady.

Aunt Patti got up, measured coffee into the filter, and inserted it into her coffee machine. She poured water into the top and switched it on.

"What does this mean?" I asked. "Do we pack stuff?

And how do we take Chase and Rainy Day? Where are we going to go? How long do things like this last?"

"I'm not sure how to answer any of those questions, April. Eat your breakfast. I'll drink my coffee. Then I'll make some more calls and figure things out. Hang tight, is what I'm saying."

I rested my bare feet on Chase's back and dug my toes into his flank. From under the table I heard his tail thump on the floor. When I was finished, I put my dishes in the dishwasher and went back to my room and lay down. As if a magician put me under a spell, I instantly fell into a deep sleep. When I awoke, my clock said 9:13. I reached over and opened *National Velvet,* another one of my mom's old books, which I had started a couple of days before. Even though some of the words were old-fashioned and hard to understand, I loved it. Velvet's whole big messy family and her crabby old pony, Miss Ada, were exactly the kind of down-to-earth country folk I had always felt alienated from, but now that I had Rainy Day, I no longer felt cut off from stories about girls and horses. Velvet seemed to be the kind of person who was both dreamy and strong, one of those girls who quietly and steadily accomplished whatever fantasy her imagination conjured up.

Just as the ten o'clock bells were ringing from the top of

the Rock and Redeemer Baptist Church, our phone rang. Aunt Patti picked up, spoke for a while, and then yelled for me. I stuck a random queen of hearts into *National Velvet* as a bookmark and got out of bed for the third time that morning. Aunt Patti hung around after passing me the phone. I could tell she was curious, because usually when a call is for me she floats out of earshot.

"April? This is Joseph McCann. You were out this way yesterday."

"Hi, Mr. McCann." I was surprised and happy to hear his voice.

"This is an awful sudden call, I know, but as I'm sure you know, Plattsburgh's having a time of it. Just about everyone I know's got troubles of their own, and I gotta barnyard of critters that need higher ground. I just plain ran out of people to call, is the truth. Old Hannah can get where she needs to go, but I need help with the rest of 'em—old Moses, the goats, and the chickens. How's about getting out here to lend me a hand? I asked your aunt and she gave her okay," he concluded on a hope-ful note.

"When do you need me?"

"Soon as you can make it. Boone's Passage is okay now, but I dunno how long it'll stay that way. You and that horse of yours should have no trouble if you come right away.

Of course I'll pay you for the trouble. And wear your work boots."

I agreed to come and hung up. Right away I thanked Aunt Patti for letting me go.

"I figure it's as good a way as any to get you and Rainy Day out of this part of town," she said. "I'll feel better when you're up on higher ground. Just promise me you'll do whatever old Joe tells you to do, hon, okay?"

"Promise. But what about you and Chase?"

"I've got a few ideas. Don't worry. I'm in touch with Marty. Use Mr. McCann's phone if you need me. It's times like this it drives me crazy that we don't have cell phone coverage out here. Might as well be on the North Pole. Anyway, when you're done, I may tell you to go straight to his place. He's up on that ridge on the other side of town."

I got dressed and packed a few things into my backpack—a toothbrush, a change of clothes, and two books. Then I went out to get Rainy Day. It was still sunny but incredibly muggy—hot and wet both. Rainy Day looked surprised to see me again so soon.

"Hey, boy, it'll be just me this time. We're going back to Mr. McCann's."

Rainy Day dipped his head for me to scratch between his ears.

"This'll give you a chance to get to know Hannah, his quarter horse. I'm sure you'll remember her."

He snorted and stomped one hoof. Then he pressed his nose against my back pocket.

"No." I laughed. "I haven't got any sugar for you right now. Maybe you can have a treat later. We'll see."

As if not believing that I didn't have any lumps of sugar or apple cubes, Rainy Day sniffed and fluttered his lips in the palm of my open hand. I patted his chin and then got busy saddling him. Within minutes, we set off for the second time that morning. Along the way, I saw people laying sandbags around their houses and in front of their first-floor windows. Obviously, people expected even more flooding.

I found Mr. McCann dragging a tub of feed across the field behind his house toward the barn.

"Hey, Mr. McCann!" I called. "Where would you like us?"

He stopped and mopped his neck with a hanky. "Good to see you, April. Why don't you set him out in that higher paddock on the other side of the house? Hannah's already there and there's water. I forget your guy's name."

"Rainy Day."

"That's right. No way to forget a name like that around here," he said ironically, walking away. "Meet me at the barn."

I unsaddled Rainy Day and slung his tack over the rail of the paddock. He immediately trotted over to greet Hannah. Almost to term with the foal she was carrying, the quarter horse mare was so wide, she practically waddled. Rainy Day and Hannah stood next to each other front to back and back to front, swishing their tails and twitching their skin. I stood watching them for a second before sprinting over to the barn.

For several hours I did whatever Mr. McCann told me to do. His creek had actually flooded the whole ground floor of his barn. Everything—including animals, feed, supplies, and tools—had to come out or get hauled up to the loft. He even had some ancient equipment that looked like junk to me but that he said was worth salvaging. We carried the chickens one by one up a hill to a higher pen, and we had to lead the goats by leashes. Old Moses was a different story.

"You can't just ask a thousand-pound pig to go wherever you want him to go," Mr. McCann said.

"We need to lure him up there," I suggested.

"Exactly."

Mr. McCann had brought out a big plastic container with a lid. I peeked in to see what was inside—bread crusts, scraps of soggy frozen waffles, shreds of bologna, brown apple cores, a rubbery fried egg, blobs of oatmeal, and mounds of limp salad. The odor was so foul, I had to turn away.

"Yuck!"

"Yuck, my foot," he said. "This here's what keeps a man of my age from overeating out of boredom. I get full, I throw whatever's on my plate into Old Moses' trough. One man's garbage is a hog's banquet. I compost out here, too. The pile's over there. My wife used to use the compost in her strawberry patch, but that was years ago. I just never got out of the habit of keeping it up."

Mr. McCann and I sprinkled the scraps into a Hansel-and-Gretel trail that led away from the barn. It was too much for old Moses to resist, and before we knew it, he was snorting and stepping his way up to higher ground.

By the middle of the afternoon we had things pretty much under control, except for one last task. Mr. McCann wanted me to take Rainy Day over to the small shed near the pond. There was a locked file box stored in the shed with some important papers that he wanted moved to a safer place.

"Here I thought that darn shed would be the best place in case a fire broke out in the main house," he said. "Now go figure. Can't get anywhere near there on two feet. A horse could. But Hannah's a little wobbly on her feet with her belly so big. Your boy could handle it."

"Sure, I'll give it a try. Rainy Day's been resting all this time and he was great in the deep water this morning."

Mr. McCann pointed me toward the pond and explained how to unfasten the shed door.

"You'll find the locked box on a low bench just inside on your right," he directed. "I'm sorry to make you do this, but that box has got the deed to this property, the title to my truck and car, and a few other documents I can't afford to lose."

"Got it," I said. "I'll be back in a bit."

I found Rainy Day and Hannah standing in the shade of a tree on the far side of the enclosure. They turned their heads as if I were interrupting their conversation and watched me approach. I led Rainy Day to the fence and saddled him. We started over to the pond, which lay down on the western side of the property opposite the main house. I couldn't locate the path Mr. McCann had pointed to because the water had risen from the creek and settled halfway up the unmowed hay of that field. Once again Rainy Day was pushing his legs through standing water that came up to his hocks. With my knees, I nudged him forward in the direction of the shed, a little prefab building that looked like it was floating on the pond.

Suddenly Rainy Day halted without my saying whoa or drawing back on the reins.

"Hey," I scolded. "You're not supposed to do that. Marty would kill me if I let you get away with that. Come on, let's go." And I gave him a cluck and a gentle but pointed nip with my heels.

Still no motion.

"I'm not kidding. We've got to get to that shed. Those papers are important. You heard Mr. McCann."

Rainy Day would not move. He shook his head vigorously from side to side as if to say no. It felt like he had turned his legs into unbudging columns of steel.

I jiggled the reins. I kicked with both feet. I clucked as loudly as I could. It was his will against mine. Everything Marty had taught me was about being the boss—and not being *afraid* to be the boss. Little did I know then that that was only a part of the lesson. Another part of the lesson was soon to come.

I pressed my hands and kicked one last time, when Rainy Day shook his whole body and reared up off his front legs. The reins fell out of my hands. As if in slow motion, I slipped out of the saddle and splashed into the water, watching Rainy Day's front legs plunge back down into the water inches away. My feet had cleared the stirrups, but I was coughing on water I had accidentally swallowed. I felt water soak into my clothes, weighing me down. I panicked that Rainy Day would lose his footing and pin me, or get his own feet tangled in the dropped reins. I paddled backwards crab-style and watched him take a small step sideways. It flashed through my mind that I had just been thrown from a horse—just like my mom. But I also knew that I was not badly hurt. I had landed pretty hard on my left knee and elbow, but otherwise I was fine. When I looked up into Rainy Day's face, it looked like he felt pity more than anything else.

"I see you're sorry now, Rainy Day," I cried, coughing more water out of my lungs. "But why in the world did you do that?"

chapter

15

"I'll need an explanation from you," I said angrily, my heart still racing as I got up from the muddy ooze of the hay field. "Exactly what makes you think you can throw me?"

Rainy Day took a step in my direction and laid his head on my shoulder. He blew against my ear as if asking to make up. The look in his eye was anything but fierce. It was apologetic.

It occurred to me that there might have been a reason for Rainy Day's stubbornness. I straightened out the reins and rested them on top of the horn of the saddle.

"Wait here a second, Rainy Day."

I sloshed forward a few paces and then, as an accidental encore, fell into a deep ditch that I hadn't noticed on account of the water level. Wet up to my armpits, I felt myself being dragged down by my sodden work boots. Then I understood. Somehow, riding through the deep water, I must have gone off the path to the shed. Luckily there were a few stones and tougher weeds that I could grab on to in order to pull up to the ridge where Rainy Day stood. I was scared again, but this time for a different reason. Had he stepped off the field into this ditch with me on his back, we both would have been seriously hurt.

"Okay, I really screwed that up," I said, remounting. "That was a close call."

Rainy Day snorted and nodded.

"You see where we need to go. Why don't you get us there the way you judge best?"

From that point on, our mission went smoothly. I opened the shed, found the locked metal box on the shelf where Mr. McCann said it would be, and lashed it behind my saddle. On the way back, I was careful to let Rainy Day find a path of his own.

At five o'clock Mr. McCann told me that Aunt Patti had called to say I should go straight to Marty's. Before I left, he thanked me and offered me a twenty-dollar bill. I didn't feel right accepting it, but Mr. McCann insisted.

"You have to take it," he said. "In all my born days I never have taken advantage of a farmhand and I don't plan on doing so today. Besides, April, here you've spent hours in those sticky, hot, wet clothes, sure as heck mighty uncomfortable, and not complainin' once."

Mr. McCann was right about that. I couldn't wait to

change, but I didn't know when I'd be getting home. Everything depended on the flooding.

From Mr. McCann's, I rode to Marty's stables. It was a climb, since his place was up on a ridge. Like everybody else in town, Marty had spent the day running around helping people and now he was finishing up his own chores. Everyone in St. Louis who stabled with him had been calling, worried about their horses. Finally, the phone had stopped ringing. We sat down in his kitchen to relax. Marty snapped open a can of soda and took a sip. He offered me one and I accepted gratefully. The can was freezing cold and I pressed it against my forehead before opening it and taking a long gulp.

"So I really messed up earlier," I said.

"How so?"

I told him how Rainy Day had not obeyed my commands. At first Marty was surprised, until I explained that it had proved to be for our own good.

"If he had done what I was urging, we would have fallen into a ditch!" I exclaimed, shaken at the thought of what might have happened. Marty nodded and polished off the rest of his soda. I blurted the question that had been bothering me all afternoon since then.

"So how do I know if he's objecting because he knows

something I don't know or if he's refusing because he's just being disobedient?"

"Well, that's the million-dollar question for people like us, now, isn't it?" Marty replied. "There's a story people tell about this very thing. It happened during World War II, which I am sure a smart girl like you has studied in school, right?" Marty raised his eyebrows expectantly.

"That's the one against Germany and Japan?"

"And Italy, right. So it was near the end of the war. The Russians, who were on our side, were battling the Germans. A terrible bloody battle, and the Germans were getting crushed. Finally they realized, 'Hey, we gotta get out of here. We need to retreat.' So what did they do? Before they turned and ran away, they buried land mines behind them as they left, so that anyone who chased them risked getting blown up."

The trail of land mines made me think of the scrap trail Mr. McCann and I had just laid for old Moses, the pig, but that one had been to lead him to safety. What Marty was talking about was pretty scary.

"It sounds like a trap," I remarked.

"That's exactly what it was. A defensive trap, you might say. So anyway, the Russian officers commanded their soldiers to chase after the retreating Germans before the Germans returned home or found a place to resupply. The Russians sent in the cavalry—the mounted troops. And the commanding Russian officer, he was a smart guy, he said, 'Let the horses have their heads, men.'"

"What?" I asked, puzzled.

"He meant, loosen up on the reins and let your horses find their own way. Let them go intuitively through this terrain, which is dotted with land mines, without any guidance from the rider. Well, some of the Russian cavalry said, no way, José. We ain't buyin' this. We'll die if we don't watch for the mines ourselves. But many of them did as their commanding officer ordered. So, April, I'm sure you can guess who made it through alive and who did not."

"Are you serious?" I asked. "Did this really happen?"

"It happened. The soldiers who trusted their mounts made it through. The ones who tried to direct the horses were blown to smithereens."

"That still doesn't answer my question," I said. "Look at a less drastic situation, like the one I was just in. How will I know when to assert my will and when to listen to his?"

"Well, I would suggest that you always listen, April," Marty said. "It's what you do with what you hear and perceive in other ways that matters. Horses will try lots of ways to get you to understand."

The kitchen phone jangled loudly. "I keep it loud so I can hear it outside," Marty explained. He got up to pluck the phone off the wall where it was mounted.

"Hello?"

It was Aunt Patti trying to track me down. She wanted me to know that we were in luck. Our house was still on solid ground, and it was okay for me to come home. I swigged the last of the soda and passed the empty can to Marty.

"Thanks," I said. "Thanks for everything."

Even though I was still a little rattled from being thrown, Rainy Day was his most easygoing self riding home. Unsaddling him back in our barn, I tried to make sense of what Marty had said. I could tell it was going to be hard for me to know for sure when to be the boss and when to trust the horse. Yet I realized that this was probably one of the most important things for me to figure out.

I mucked out his stall and poured fresh water in his trough. I scooped a bunch of oats into his bin and mixed in two scoops of corn. Once he was content in his stall eating, I brought over the grooming supplies. He had loads of pebbly mud and clumps of grass stuck on the bottoms of his feet. Each hoof took a long while to get clean. I found myself apologizing to him as I worked.

"I should have trusted you that time," I said aloud. "I just wasn't listening."

I didn't hear anything back from Rainy Day—only the sound of his teeth grinding through the snack and a quiet muffled stomp now and then. I continued to groom him. Mentally, I was in a peaceful but attentive zone, going through the motions that were becoming second nature to me. As I pressed the currycomb through the caked mud along his sides, a distinct voice came surging up from my memory.

> *Oh, don't you want just one little bite, sweetie pie?*
> *This is yummy mashed potato and squash, my girl. Yes,*
> *you are Mommy's precious little April. How about*
> *tasting one little yummy bite? You usually gobble this*
> *up. I wonder why you won't open your mouth and take*
> *even one little bite. You can't be full already, can you?*

I knew exactly what I was listening to. The infant was me, sitting in a high chair. The person talking was my mom. She was feeding me, or trying to. I kept turning my head away and clamping my lips closed.

And there I was a few minutes later, flushed and goggle-eyed from throwing up all over the high-chair tray and my mom's shirt. I could practically taste the vomit.

Oh, April, you poor thing! You must have picked up a bug. Stupid me. Let's put this food away and get you cleaned up and feeling better.

The reason I wasn't eating was because I was sick. I just didn't have the words to explain that to my mom. So she kept putting that potato-squash mash in my mouth until eventually I threw up. Then she knew, all right.

The memory made me smile. It also made me think. This was the exact same situation I had been in with Rainy Day earlier that day. Just as my mom hadn't understood that I was clamping my mouth shut and turning away because I was sick, I hadn't understood that Rainy Day was trying to make a sensible decision, too. Some of those Russian soldiers in Marty's story made the same mistake—with much more terrible consequences.

From now on, I would have to make sure that my intuition was tuned in to *his* intuition. I would have to do my best to make my hunches line up with his. Then instead of me always telling Rainy Day what to do, our communication would go both ways, just like that book

Open Channels suggested. It all boiled down to trust, I thought, brushing the last tangles out of Rainy Day's tail.

I stood up and finished the evening chores without another word.

chapter

16

The flooding stabilized over the rest of Sunday afternoon and evening, and Monday morning I got up and went to school as usual. The only difference was that we had a late start. Instead of the first bell ringing at 8:05, it rang an hour later. Of course, the flood was all anyone could talk about in class. And it seemed like every single teacher had planned some kind of lesson based on what was happening around us.

Mr. Millstadt, the social studies teacher, talked about the flood of 1993. That was the year when the Mississippi came all the way up to the base of the Arch in St. Louis and the Missouri swelled across Chesterfield Valley. He mentioned how trying to control these powerful river systems and building houses and malls in what he called the most fertile floodplain in the Western Hemisphere was, in his opinion, just plain stupid. But we were all used to Mr. Millstadt's rants, and a lot of kids tuned out and passed notes.

Our science teacher, Ms. Finnegan, gave a speech on

the water cycle. The one thing I remember best from science that day was Ms. Finnegan's saying that we needed to stay alert to this situation, because while the water had stopped rising, the ground was still supersaturated.

"Any additional rainfall will mean the worst is still to come," she said ominously.

During lunch and free periods, kids started talking about what they had experienced. I could not believe some of the stories I heard. At one end of the cafeteria, Lowell had an audience of nine or ten kids hanging on his every word. As I passed by with my tray, I heard the jeering voice of this mean kid in our grade, David Faust.

"Dude, why go to all that trouble for a cat?"

David tried to get the other kids to laugh along with him, but it wound up backfiring because most people thought David was kind of a jerk. Eventually he shuffled out to the yard.

After the last bell, I met up with Lowell. Without any discussion or plan, we headed home together, both of us glad to return to our old routine. Along the way, I noticed a rust-colored paste on the sidewalk. Someone at school said that when the water receded over the last twenty-four hours, it had left behind a layer of sediment. And that wasn't the only result of the flood. Branches, leaves, garbage, and debris were strewn around in weird places—on roofs, in tree limbs, and between fence posts. Chain saws whined in every direction as home owners began the enormous process of cleaning up. Plattsburgh was in shambles.

I complained to Lowell about my C on the last pre-algebra test of the year. He told me he had gotten an A. This was a big deal—an A meant that he had decided to study for the test, which meant that he had decided that it mattered to study, which meant that he had decided that there was a point to learning math in seventh grade. All year long I had watched him either goof off, zone out, or be rude in class. Lowell must have packed an entire year's worth of material into a few nights of cramming.

"That's amazing," I said.

Lowell shrugged, as though the accomplishment was all in a day's work.

We went to his house to hang out for a while. I was surprised to see both his parents at the kitchen table. Lowell may have been surprised, too, but he didn't show it.

"Hey, Mom. Hey, Dad."

Miz Fran stood up and gave me a hug. "April, I feel like I haven't seen you for ages. I see you coming and going with that horse—"

"Rainy Day."

"Rainy Day. And Lowell told me what happened yesterday morning. It's crazy, isn't it?"

Miz Fran got up and brought over a bowl of corn chips and a plastic container of creamy artichoke dip. After a look at that snack, Lowell opened the fridge and got out a bag of miniature carrots. I guess he had been "making healthy choices" in his eating habits, as our P.E. teacher would say. Exercising, dieting—what was next for Lowell in the personal transformation department?

"Speaking of current events, Lowell, your dad has some good news."

Mr. Walt laughed. "Yeah. For a change."

"What is it, Dad?"

"Sit down and I'll tell you. April, you look more grown-up every day," he said.

"Thanks, but I don't really think I do. People who don't know me assume I'm in fifth grade. I'm still the shortest girl in the class," I said, resigned.

"No, he's right, April," Miz Fran said. "There's something about the expression on your face that looks more mature. It's not your height or anything physical like that. Anyway, Walt, go on."

Mr. Walt looked at Lowell.

"The county called me up and asked if I would supervise the crews cleaning up the mess around here," he said. "They want me to start immediately. They got my name from an old supervisor at Chrysler. They said Plattsburgh and the towns around here aren't set up to deal with the flooding, and that if I wanted to, with all my so-called expertise as a machinist, they'd hire me to manage a whole new section of public works just for this kind of thing. What kinds of tools and machines we need to buy, who should run 'em, when and how to deploy them."

"That's terrific, Mr. Walt!" I said.

I could tell Lowell was relieved, but his face was still guarded, as if he didn't want to fall for anything that would turn out to be a disappointment in the end.

Mr. Walt seemed to read Lowell's mind.

"It'll be nice to tackle some real problems for a change," he said. "And get paid to do it. I've probably been spending too much time yelling about problems that aren't really problems."

I hoped Mr. Walt would stop there.

Miz Fran put her hand on top of Mr. Walt's and looked at Lowell with a sad sort of smile. I felt like it was time for me to go.

"Thanks for the snack. Congratulations, Mr. Walt. See

you, Lowell." I waved, heading toward the door.

"Oh, April, why don't you join us for dinner? We'd love to have you, and Lowell's been spending so much time at your house. I'll call Patti and invite her, too."

"Thanks, Miz Fran, but I've got to do my evening chores in the barn. Plus, Aunt Patti asked me to help her with some yard work. She's freaked out about her mums and root rot and all that."

I left and went straight to Rainy Day. I was happy for Lowell, and for his family, but I also felt sad and lonesome. The way Lowell and his parents sat there in their little circle—father, mother, and child—was a reminder that I would never get to experience that feeling.

The minute I began taking care of Rainy Day, cheerier feelings took over the sadness. He had been waiting for me to get home and was happy to see me. Watching his body language—his ears, the expression in his eyes, the turn of his head—I could tell he enjoyed every single reassuring touch and sound.

"You know, Rainy Day," I said, rubbing him down one of his front legs, "I try to remember when my parents were alive, but it's hard. I was only four years old when they died, did I ever tell you that?"

Rainy Day lowered his leg and I walked around to his

other side, trailing one hand across his chest.

"I try so hard to remember moments that are not frozen pictures in photo albums. See, it always bothered me that that's all I had—pictures. I wanted to remember whole moments. Actual feelings. I wanted to know the daily boring details of everyday life with them. Not having that is what gives me a gaping empty feeling sometimes. Not even to know what I missed."

Rainy Day blurred in front of me. I fought back tears so I could keep going.

"But it's so complicated," I said. "I mean, I love Aunt Patti so much, and I wouldn't trade my life with anyone's for anything. But it's like I want both. I want what I have and I want what was taken away."

I thought about the story Marty told about my mom and me in the barn. Even a little snippet like that made me realize how much I craved those stories. Maybe that's what had triggered the memory of me in the high chair. Surely I must have more of those memories stored up somewhere in my brain. I pressed my face against Rainy Day's firm, warm shoulder. It was like he was my life raft and I was hanging on for dear life. Chores or no chores, I couldn't hold it back any longer. I started to cry against Rainy Day's strong side. I don't know how long it had been since I had sobbed so hard, but there was nothing I could do now to stop. Eventually I pulled myself together and said, "That's it, April. Stop crying. You've got chores and homework to do."

Rainy Day turned his head to look at me calmly. At the sound of a cawing crow outside he nickered quietly. Then he nosed my back pocket. I laughed.

"Oh, all right. Here you go." I reached over to the bucket of cut carrots and let him nibble one out of my palm.

I sat down at the small worktable in the corner and made my day's entry in the log. I noted the amount of feed Rainy Day ate that day, how many miles he had walked the day before, and in what gaits. I made a note that Rainy Day had carried not just my 103 pounds but also Lowell, who probably weighed around 150. Also, I wrote about Rainy Day's experience with Hannah over at the McCann place. I was so engrossed in recording this information that I didn't hear Aunt Patti's car pull into the driveway, or that it had begun to rain again softly.

chapter

That night I hung out in the kitchen and helped Aunt Patti make dinner. Chase slept on his beat-up cushion by the back door. While I washed lettuce, Aunt Patti tossed nine raw chicken legs in a bowl and poured a bottle of French dressing over them. Once they were coated in the orange-red marinade, she spread them on a cookie sheet and put them in the oven. Then she started on the rice. She had the radio tuned to the eighties station and was dancing from place to place along the counter—sort of sashaying her hips and rocking her shoulders in time with the music. We both sang along with the radio even though neither of us knew the words, except for the catchy choruses.

"Aunt Patti, did you and Dad and your brothers and sisters fight a lot?"

"Some, just like kids in all families, I guess. Your uncle Jimmy, he could say mean things that he knew would hurt your feelings. And Aunt Becky pinched. But your dad never did anything like that. He and I were always the closest. We even had a secret club." She laughed. "The

River Rovers. Of course, we were the only two members—well, us and a pretend friend we called Gorloff."

"Gorloff?"

"I guess it sounds pretty dumb now. But Gorloff was kind of a half-giant, half-wizard. He was in our power and nobody knew he existed except us. Anyway, the River Rovers were responsible for making the sun rise and set every day. Your dad signaled to Gorloff to push the sun down at night, and I signaled him to lift it up in the morning. We also made hidden camps down along the St. Jeanne branch of the Bourbeuse River. You can laugh, April, but we took our adventures very seriously. Gorloff also kept a running list of the people who we decided were good and the people we decided were bad. He did a lot of erasing and rewriting, because these lists changed daily, sometimes hourly. You can go on and set the table, please."

As we talked, I arranged pairs of forks, knives, spoons, napkins, plates, and glasses on the table. The water had gone down in the small bud vase in the middle of the table so I carried it to the sink and added more water to it.

"Did my parents ever talk about having more kids?" I asked. "I mean, that you know of?"

Aunt Patti didn't answer right away. I figured she probably didn't know, but I was wrong.

"One Christmas, when you must have been no older than two, your mom and I were talking. You were running around flushed and crazy with your cousins, and your dad was helping in the kitchen. Anyway, I remember Mary Beth asking me about school—what I planned to major in, how my courses were. At some point in that conversation she told me that she and your dad knew that one child was enough for them. They loved you so much and took such good care of you, April. Your mom sat there beaming, just watching you play, and she said, 'I think we're just right as we are, Patti. April will have cousins all her life, and the life we've got in Plattsburgh, running Ozark Pastures, feels like what I'm meant to do. And in a way, April *will* have...'"

"What? April will have what?" I demanded. "What did she say I would have?"

Aunt Patti got up and went over to the counter. She picked up a dish towel and absently wiped a drop of marinade. Then she reached into the salad bowl and tore a large piece of lettuce in half.

"No fair, Aunt Patti," I whined. "Finish your sentence. April will have..."

She turned back around to face me.

"It's just that I had forgotten this part of our conversation until this very moment. She said something like, 'In a way, April *will* have brothers and sisters; they'll just have manes and tails.' Little did she know."

"You mean little did she know that I would spend nine years freaked out about horses?"

"I guess. Although plenty of people get back together with estranged siblings over time. It's a case of better late than never."

Aunt Patti looked at me and smiled.

"And what about you?" I asked. "I mean, here you are, with me. Obviously, it's not what you expected."

"Nope. It's not." She put down her fork and knife and reached out to squeeze my hand. "But sometimes the best experiences in the world are the ones you don't expect. I think that's what finally dissolved the River Rovers. We got bored with our power, you know, making the same thing happen twice a day every single day."

"So what happened to Gorloff?" I asked.

"Beats me. I guess he started hanging out with some other kids." She shrugged and we both laughed.

After dinner we went into the living room. Aunt Patti pulled out her scrapbook materials and I turned on the television. Nothing good was on and I had a couple of finals to study for. I kissed Aunt Patti good night and went off to my room.

Eventually I closed my textbooks and got into bed with *National Velvet*. I was getting near the end, when Velvet has won the Grand National and the family is being swarmed by newspaper reporters. I turned the page and a scrap of yellowed lined paper fluttered down onto my chest. I picked up the piece of paper and saw a letter on one side scrawled in cursive handwriting.

To Whom It May Concern:

I, Mary Beth Flagel, do sollumly swear to uphold the happiness of horses everywhere as long as I live. I also promisss to stop steeling food like shugar and apples from the kitchen and taking it to the barn because I know that I should ask permmission first.

Signed, Mary Beth FlagelMarch 14, 1974

My mom must have been reading *National Velvet* when she was overcome by the desire to declare her official promise. I wondered how old she was then. Born in 1967, she would have been around seven. Seven years old and already knowing exactly what she would do with her life. Seven years old and already a thief, not to mention a bad speller.

I lay in bed staring at that little scrap of paper. I had

never thought about my parents as children before—as actual kids. In my head they had been frozen in time, forever the couple who other people knew as "April Helmbach's parents, who died in a freak accident."

Chase tick-tacked on long toenails into my room and jumped onto the end of my bed. He nosed forward to sniff at the paper in my hand and then curled himself into a ring beside my feet. I closed the book and turned off my light.

I drifted off to sleep and began to dream right away. But my dreams that night were very strange—they took place at different times and places, but appeared as scenes linked together. In the first dream I was looking up at the blades of a helicopter chopping through the sky and coming down toward my face. Somebody was holding me too tight and I tried to scramble away. Dust bit into my eyes as I watched something get lifted up and carried away into the blue sky. Then that scene merged into one where I was at the top of the Arch. My grandma was holding me steady as I peered out the window looking east.

> *Where's Mommy? Where's Daddy?*
> *Look out this window, April. You can see all the way*
> *across Illinois. And come over here to the other side.*
> *See if you can see all the way to Plattsburgh.*
> *Where's Mommy and Daddy?*

Next Chase and I were at my grandma's house in St. Louis. She had made me a bowl of poached eggs mixed with crushed crackers. I finished my lunch and got down on the floor with my dress-up dolls. I was changing the doll's shoes because I liked green better than pink. Aunt Patti's face came close to mine and she lifted me up. I yanked on her curly black ponytail and she squeezed me tight. I looked into her shiny black eyes, put my hand on her chin, and listened as she spoke with Grandma. Uncle Jimmy was down on the floor on his hands and knees. He wanted to give me a horsey-back ride but I started to cry. Aunt Patti yelled at him and started crying, too.

In the last dream I was lying in a big bed with Aunt Patti, watching a nature show about lemurs. Snuggled next to the warm flannel of her nightie, I fell asleep.

The sensation of falling asleep in my dream snapped me awake.

Something seemed different, as if a long dark tunnel had been lit by radiant sunshine. I no longer felt like a branch cut off from a tree—lonesome and left out. What had happened to my parents was terrible, of course, but deep down I had always believed that it had been most terrible for me. It seemed obvious now that the accident had been most disastrous for my mom and dad. They were the ones who were cut off from us. I was lucky. I had Aunt Patti. I had family in St. Louis—my grandma, my cousins, and my aunts and uncles. I had Lowell and my other friends at school. I had Chase. I had Rainy Day. I had my life.

After this realization, I finally fell into a dreamless, sound sleep. It was the kind of sleep where you close your eyes at night and open them in the morning, with no sensation that any time has passed in between.

chapter

The next three days went by quickly. It had been sunny, so everyone assumed that the worst of the weather was behind us.

I took the rest of my exams, bought a two-piece bathing suit for the summer, and got my braces off. Rainy Day and I went out for a few long rides, mostly over to Mr. McCann's house to check on his animals but also to Marty's for riding lessons. I had progressed quickly and undramatically from trotting to cantering, but Marty had said that was typical of novice riders.

"The canter's an easier gait to control than the trot. Smoother, more comfortable for the horse."

"So then how about I gallop?" I said.

"Not on your life," he said. "You gallop, you flirt with the horse's instinct to run for his life. You're nowhere near ready to deal with a runaway horse."

Thursday, the last day of school, rolled around. We spent the morning cleaning out our lockers, packing up our gym clothes, getting yearbooks signed, and talking about our summer plans. Our school always served an outdoor barbecue lunch on the last day, so at noon kids were sitting on blankets around the yard, enjoying the sunshine.

I was just finishing my last potato chip when I noticed a dark shadow fall across the yard. By the end of lunch period, a solid mass of gray clouds had moved in from the west and the first heavy drops of rain began to fall. Everybody jumped up. We threw away our trash and ran back inside. A half hour later it was pouring. A schoolwide announcement went out over the intercom.

"Attention all students, teachers, and staff. This is Mrs. Clifford. We have decided to dismiss school an hour early this afternoon. The school bus service has informed me that the roads around Plattsburgh are likely to wash out in this rain, and we want to see everyone get home safely. I am sorry that this has to happen on the last day of school, but these are events beyond our control. Please report directly to your homerooms and listen for the dismissal announcements. You will be called by bus assignment. Those of you who walk to school may sign out and leave at this time."

I met up with Lowell by the front door and we headed for home together. Luckily, I had found a crumpled old sweatshirt in my gym locker so I hunched under the hood. Lowell had found a black garbage bag, which he used to cover his backpack. Still, by the time we got to my house, we were soaked. Not to mention shocked. Our neighborhood was downhill from school, and the creeks were already swollen.

Aunt Patti came rushing in the door at the same time we did.

"You kids can fix yourselves a snack," she said. "I've shut up my shop for the rest of the day. Everyone downtown is bracing for the worst. This could be a long night. Have you seen the news?"

Aunt Patti flipped on the weather report. She moaned when she saw that the forecast showed nothing but rain for the next day or two. Lowell and I toasted two cinnamon swirl buns and ate them with milk. Aunt Patti called into the kitchen.

"April, Lowell! Get in here. Lowell, your dad's on TV."

It was true. Mr. Walt was being interviewed by the KPOM reporter. He asked Lowell's dad what measures were being taken by the officials in Plattsburgh to manage the flooding. Mr. Walt looked grim.

"First off, we've blockaded all the large and small bridges in town," he replied. "We don't want people trying to cross even the smaller creeks. In the event of a flash flood, people shouldn't be anywhere near a bridge. Second, we've got road crews outside as we speak, laying sandbags along the levees of the Bourbeuse and some of the larger tributaries. Third, all the drainage systems in town have been cleared of debris in the last few days, so the water that can flow into the sewer system *will* flow into the sewer system."

Aunt Patti stood watching with one hand on her hip, the remote control in the other.

"I think your dad's got his hands full, Lowell," she said. "We won't be seeing much of him, it sounds like. Call your mom and tell her to come on over once she's boarded up your house. I've got to go see about our own papers and things."

Aunt Patti went into her room.

"I'm going to go home instead of call," Lowell said. "Could be my mom needs me to help out. We'll come back as soon as we can."

"Okay," I said as Lowell headed for the door. I was trying to organize my thoughts. "I think I'll pack up some clothes for me and food for Chase. Then I'll go out and make sure Rainy Day's dry and get him ready in case we need to leave."

After Lowell left, I organized things in the house with

Aunt Patti. At four o'clock I went out to the barn. Rainy Day shook his head and waved his tail, happy to see me. I offered him a palm full of corn, which he nibbled right out of my hand. But he kept stomping his feet, one after the other, as if something was bothering him. I didn't see any flies, and there was nothing on his skin. The only noise around was the steady beat of rain on the tin roof over our heads.

"What is it, Rainy Day? What is it, boy?"

I rubbed his side and under his chin, but nothing I did settled him. I had never seen him so agitated and nervous.

"I'll be back in a little while," I said reassuringly. "This has got to end at some point."

Back in the house I knocked on Aunt Patti's bedroom door. Normally she never closed her door.

"Come in."

"Hey. What are you up to?" I asked, starting to feel anxious.

"I just don't want all this stuff to be destroyed if..."

"If what? You mean, if our house washes away?" I joked, but Aunt Patti didn't laugh.

She was squatting on the floor of her closet, going through what looked like piles of junk. It turned out to be letters and papers.

"It's all my stuff from college—transcripts and term papers. I don't want to lose these things. A lot of it is still at Grandma's, but a bunch of it's here—letters, too, from your dad and old boyfriends. Pictures that didn't make it into albums. I'm going to get it together and put it on top of the refrigerator. By the way, I want you to go shut down the computer. What's the highest place in the house where we can put it temporarily?"

It was starting to sink in that things might get worse before they got better. The phone kept ringing, and I heard Aunt Patti reassuring people one after another that we were fine, that we had things under control. Eventually she snapped at Grandma, who seemed to call every fifteen minutes.

"Mom, we are fine," I heard Aunt Patti say through tight lips. "Please, just let me handle this and I will call you as soon as things settle down. April is fine. Here, you talk to her."

"Hi, Grandma . . . Yes. No, it's just raining really hard . . . Fine . . . Yes . . . I will . . . I will . . . Love you, too . . . Bye." I hung up.

"Grandma says to tell you to use your head and come over to her house as soon as the roads are open again."

Aunt Patti snorted.

At seven o'clock we turned up the volume on the TV because there was a new announcement crawling along the bottom of the screen.

WARNING: FLASH FLOODS REPORTED IN WARREN COUNTY AND UNION COUNTY. DOZENS OF BRIDGES AND ROADS WASHED AWAY. TRAVEL UNADVISED UNTIL FURTHER NOTICE. WARNING: NINE INCHES OF RAIN HAVE FALLEN IN PLATTSBURGH SINCE TWO O'CLOCK TODAY. FLASH FLOODS REPORTED THROUGHOUT PLATTSBURGH COUNTY.

"Here we go, April," Aunt Patti said. "I think we can definitely call this an emergency."

Someone banged on our front door. Aunt Patti opened it. Lowell and Miz Fran stomped water off their shoes and came inside.

"Have you heard about the trailer park down on Christina and Jefferson?" Miz Fran said.

"No, what about it?" Aunt Patti asked.

"Mrs. Baumsdorf called me up to say that she heard that the water down there's moving so fast, a couple of those trailers have come loose and are being knocked over by the current," Miz Fran explained.

"Isn't everyone already evacuated from there? I heard they all left last week," Aunt Patti said, gesturing for Miz Fran to sit down and make herself comfortable.

"Well, evacuation was optional. I don't know if everyone got out." Miz Fran collapsed onto the sofa. "And I think some people who did go may have come back."

"But that's where Shawn lives," I said, feeling a pang in the pit of my stomach.

"Shawn who?" Miz Fran asked.

"This guy I met at the library. He's in a wheelchair. He's an Iraq vet," I added.

"What if he didn't move when people were told to?"

"I'm not sure we can do anything about it," Aunt Patti said. "But who is this guy anyway?"

"It'll take too long to explain," I said. "He could be in trouble now."

"What makes you think he's alone?" Miz Fran asked. "Do you have his phone number or any other way to reach him?"

Speechless, I shook my head no. Then I started to blurt, "His mom's away. He's friends with the librarian. He's sort of college age, more or less."

"How about I page my dad?" Lowell suggested, trying to make me feel better.

"I guess you can try," I said.

"Fran, while the kids are tracking down Walt, could you help me move the computer? I've got all my records for the shop here at home. I just can't lose all my work. It's in my room."

Aunt Patti and Miz Fran hurried down the hall into Aunt Patti's bedroom.

I got my boots on and grabbed my poncho off the coat tree by the front door.

Lowell finished paging his dad and looked up.

"April, what are you doing?"

"Shhh," I hissed, not wanting Aunt Patti to hear. "I'm going to make sure Shawn's okay."

"Are you crazy? You can't do that. The trailer park's completely flooded. Remember how bad it was the other day? It's going to be worse now. Let me try my dad again," he said, reaching for the cordless.

"Your dad's going to be busy, Lowell. He's got a million other things to worry about. You'll know where I am. If I'm not back in an hour, send help." With that I was out the door.

I ran to the barn and rushed inside. Rainy Day had been nickering for a while, I guess, but in the rain I hadn't heard him. Even though it was only ten after seven, nowhere close to dark on normal days, it seemed like sunset. The clouds overhead were thick and gray, heavy with falling rain. I was glad that I had anticipated this kind of emergency and that I had already saddled Rainy Day. He seemed eager to get outside even under such lousy conditions. I mounted him in the driveway, and we walked to the north in the direction of the trailer park.

Most of the stores we passed were boarded up and the houses looked empty and dark. Rainy Day waded gingerly across huge puddles, unsure of what might be on the bottom.

Conditions grew worse as we approached Christina Street, the place where three main creeks came together. Instead of walking from puddle to puddle, we were now trudging through a newly formed shallow lake with no end in sight. Like the other day, the water was swirling around Rainy Day's knees.

Suddenly I heard someone shouting. I looked in the direction of the voice and was amazed to see a stocky woman balanced on a tire swing and clutching desperately at the rope. I recognized her as the person behind the counter at the gas station where we usually filled up. The water came up to the bottom of the tire, enveloping her lower legs entirely. Then I heard another voice coming from the same direction. Above the swing was another woman perched on the branch from which the tire swing hung. The two women were shouting at each other, and the big woman below was sobbing. From where I sat, they actually seemed secure in their bizarre positions, as long as the water didn't rise any higher.

"I'll get help!" I shouted. The women didn't hear me. I wasn't even sure they could see me. I made a mental note to remember where they were and kept going.

Closer to the trailer park, I brought Rainy Day to a halt because large pieces of debris were cruising by us in the water—a blue plastic inflatable kiddy pool, a watering can, tin buckets, an uncoiled green hose, clumps of leaves, and large dead branches. Twenty yards ahead, I saw a rusty silver propane tank the size of a bathtub bobbing along half-submerged. It flowed in the current toward the fix-it shop at the east end of the park two blocks away. Within seconds, the tank smashed into the brick wall of the fix-it shop and exploded in flames.

Rainy Day tried to rear, but the water was too deep. I held on to the reins and squeezed my legs into his sides.

"Steady, boy. Steady, Rainy Day. We need to keep going."

I heard a siren blast and wondered if that was a fire

truck or the emergency signal for the whole town. Before we could advance, I saw a full-size trailer slide by us, tipped halfway onto its side. I prayed nobody was inside.

I urged Rainy Day forward to where the rest of the trailers were parked. Some were rocking. Others were spinning around in slow circles. Everywhere I looked screamed disaster. A trailer might have come loose and run over us. Floating debris and branches could have ensnared us. Another propane tank might have exploded beside us, but all I could think about was Shawn trapped in his wheelchair, unable to get away. I started calling his name, louder and louder over the sounds of whooshing rain and gushing water that surrounded us.

Suddenly I felt different in the saddle. The whole rhythm of Rainy Day's movements had changed. There was a churning feeling under me.

"Oh, my gosh, you're swimming, aren't you? You're actually swimming."

My feet were completely underwater and beginning to go numb with cold. I could barely feel my hands as they gripped the reins, which I held tightly even though I was giving Rainy Day full freedom of head movement. My legs squeezed tight into his sides as I scanned the area for signs of human life.

"Where is he, Rainy Day?"

I wiped water away from my eyes to see better.

"APRIL!! IS THAT YOU?!?"

I turned and saw the very top of a narrow green street sign. It said CHRISTINA. All the rest of the pole was underwater.

"April! Over here!"

In his wheelchair, Shawn was sitting in the doorway of the trailer. He was waving his arms wildly, one hand holding a red Cardinals baseball cap. Although he looked like he was yelling at the top of his lungs, I could barely hear him. There was no sign of the concrete blocks the trailer sat on, or of the ramp that led up to the door. Even the wheelchair was half-submerged. Shawn's lower legs were underwater.

"SHAWN!"

I pulled the reins to the right over Rainy Day's withers but he didn't seem to change course. He actually seemed to be heading away from Shawn. I tried again.

"Rainy Day, we need to go over there," I pleaded, fighting back tears. "See? See where Shawn is? There! OVER THERE!"

Rainy Day continued churning under me. With water swirling around us, I couldn't tell whether we were moving in any direction at all. How could I make Rainy Day do what I wanted?

Then I remembered what had happened at Mr. McCann's and Marty's story about the Russian cavalry.

"I get it, Rainy Day," I said, leaning forward toward his ears. "You're avoiding something I can't see in this muddy water. Is that it, buddy?"

I closed my eyes and let the reins fall loose in my hands.

"Please, Rainy Day, please just go over to Shawn as soon as you can."

When I opened my eyes again, I saw that he had made a wide half circle and was now pedaling his legs toward the trailer. We were getting closer and closer to Shawn, who now had water up to his lap.

"April!" he shouted. "Can you get just a little bit closer? If I could just reach the saddle…"

"I'm trying. Wait. Hang on."

Rainy Day maneuvered us alongside the flooded porch.

"There!" Shawn exploded, hurling himself up and out of the wheelchair.

I felt a sudden pressure behind my back. Shawn had one hand gripping the back of the saddle and the other wrapped across Rainy Day's rump. He was grunting and swearing. I was afraid of losing my balance if I turned completely around, but I could see Shawn's legs off to the side, dangling and floating on the surface of the water.

"You've got to climb completely on," I shouted.

"I'm trying, I'm trying." I couldn't turn around, but I heard Shawn mutter a long string of swear words as he struggled into a secure position.

Meanwhile, Rainy Day was moving along toward the higher ground where Christina meets State Street.

"I can't do it," Shawn said. "I need more leverage to get up and over. I'll have to stay like this. At least this way my legs won't get in the way of your horse's."

I was barely holding the reins at all, just enough so they didn't fall to either side of Rainy Day's face and tangle him up. With a sudden jerk, I felt his hooves meet solid ground, which told me he was walking instead of swimming. Then I heard a giant grunt from behind, one more loud set of swears and oaths, and felt Shawn upright behind me. Both his legs hung off to one side so that he sat sidesaddle. Once I could see the road under Rainy Day's hooves I took up the reins and patted him on the neck. "You did it, Rainy Day," I said.

"Strange times for Army Specialist Clarke," Shawn said, shifting his weight behind me. "Who'd have ever thought

I'd get my butt out of Iraq only to nearly drown in Plattsburgh, Missouri?"

chapter

Night had fallen by the time we reached my house. Aunt Patti was out on our front porch with a flashlight in one hand and the phone in the other. Our transistor radio sat on the porch rail. Her dark curly hair was a wet mess, with clumped strands plastered across her cheek, and her expression I can only describe as a mixture of fury, worry, relief, and shock.

"April!" she said angrily, watching us approach.

"I'm sorry," I said, bringing Rainy Day to a halt by the barn door, where she had run out to meet us. "You know you would have said no if I had asked."

I could tell she was trying to decide which way to go— outraged guardian or proud and relieved aunt. Aunt Patti looked at me, then at Shawn sitting behind me in the saddle.

"This is Shawn, the guy I mentioned? From the library? He was stuck down there after all."

"Ma'am," Shawn said, more humble than I had ever heard him.

Quickly, before dismounting, I explained what had happened and where we had been. I also mentioned the two women I had seen in the tire swing and tree. Rainy Day rubbed a hoof on the gravel of the driveway.

For the moment, proud aunt won out.

"I heard about them just now on the radio," Aunt Patti said, stepping closer and patting Rainy Day on the side of his neck. "They're all right, too, thank heavens. One of their neighbors actually took out his rowboat and got them down."

She looked up at me and spoke softly. "April, you took advantage of your freedom. You see that, right? I don't have to tell you that you put me through a pretty terrible experience just now."

Rainy Day's head was hanging and white froth foamed from the corners of his mouth. He was exhausted and so was I. When I swung off his back, my legs sort of wobbled like jelly under me for a second. Finding my balance, I hugged Aunt Patti and whispered, "I'm really, really sorry. But what if I hadn't gone?"

We looked at each other for a second and then she smiled, her eyes glazed over with tears.

I turned and took out Rainy Day's bit.

"Yoo-hoo down there. How about I get off this angel of

mercy?" Shawn said. "I can wait on the driveway here while you take care of the noble steed."

Aunt Patti was still too emotional to laugh.

"Let me run over and get Lowell," she said. "Power's out all over town. He's just sitting in the dark with his mom, but I'm sure he'd want to give us a hand getting you inside, Shawn."

While Aunt Patti was getting Lowell, I tied Rainy Day to his hitching post and brought over his water bucket so he could take a long drink. Shawn watched from his sidesaddle perch.

"Sorry about my cursing back there," he said. "I don't know what to say or how to thank you. I'd be fish food by now if you hadn't showed up."

"It's okay," I said. "It's not like I have never heard language like that. Although I have to admit, your swearing is rather—"

"Creative?"

"I guess. Creative, more than what I normally hear."

Aunt Patti returned with Lowell and we considered making a seat with our interlinked arms for Shawn to sit in, but Lowell said it would be easier for him to just carry Shawn piggyback into the house. He turned around and Shawn slid down off Rainy Day. Lowell carted him off, with Aunt Patti lighting the way with the flashlight.

I patted Rainy Day all over. His body was overheated and soaking wet. What he needed was a long cool-off and then a thorough grooming. I looked up. The clouds were breaking apart, revealing a sliver of moon against the dark evening sky. Grooming Rainy Day would be difficult, if not impossible, without electric light. I led him inside the stall and did the best I could. Picking out his hooves, I basically handled them as if I were blind, my fingers feeling their way. By the time I was done and Rainy Day was crunching on a tub of fresh oats, I felt a little dizzy. I sat down in a corner and closed my eyes. When Aunt Patti came out to see where I was, she found me sound asleep on a pile of clean saddle pads.

The next morning, all of Plattsburgh was declared to be in a state of emergency. We still had no electricity, so we listened to the news on the transistor radio. Aunt Patti and I had moved everything out of the refrigerator into a couple of coolers. But we lucked out: The water at our place had never come higher than our top porch step.

When I woke up, Aunt Patti and Shawn were in the living room, eating peach yogurts and drinking coffee.

Sunshine streamed through the open windows. The night before, Lowell had brought over a pair of gym shorts and a dry T-shirt for Shawn to change into. The borrowed clothes made him look much younger than he did in his tough-looking camo shirt.

"Shawn's been telling me how things got so bad so quickly down there," Aunt Patti said.

"I hadn't realized everyone was gone until it was too late," Shawn said. "I've been in some weird situations, but that was the weirdest yet. That neighbor of yours, Lowell, he told me that he heard all the drainage systems in town just collapsed, which has to be what made it even worse. There was no place for the water to go."

"Lowell's dad had said that would be the worst-case scenario," Aunt Patti said. "Now they're trying to open up all those systems and actually dig out more runoff catches."

"I'm just glad that most of my belongings aren't in that trailer," Shawn said. "I've been spending most of my time up at the library. All my books and files are stored on the computer up there. I do wonder where the wheelchair ended up."

"I bet it'll turn up," Aunt Patti said.

I went into the kitchen and got myself a cherry yogurt and a spoon. I came back in and plopped down on the couch next to Shawn. I was glad he didn't gush with thanks and gratitude, and that Aunt Patti didn't make me tell the whole story again from beginning to end, which would have made me feel awkward and uncomfortable. I was glad that we could go on from where we were.

"What else have we got to eat?" I said.

"You can make a PB and J," Aunt Patti said.

"I'll take one of those if you're dealing them out," Shawn said.

After we ate, I went out to the barn to visit Rainy Day. In the light of day, I could see how tangled his bangs still were. They dangled in a mess to one side, making him look almost Goth. His tail was matted. Other than that, he seemed no worse for the experience. I kissed his nose and pulled up his lips to make sure nothing had gotten stuck in his mouth or between his teeth while he had been swimming.

"Kind of an intense look you've got going there, buddy," I said. "I guess I really couldn't see what I was doing. Anyway, we should go see your friends at Shady Glen, as soon as things settle down. Meanwhile, let's fix you back up."

I gave him fresh hay and got a bucket of water. It took me a while to clean the grit out of his bangs and tail, which had dried to a hard muddy cake. I put the tools away and went back into the house. At first Aunt Patti didn't want to let me ride up to Shady Glen, but I reminded her that it was up out of the valley and probably never weathered any flash floods at all.

"Besides," I said, "there's nothing much to do around here. Except talk, of course. You can't go to work, and school's out."

"April," she said, "do me a favor and wait a couple of hours to make sure the roads are open. There's no hurry, and it wouldn't hurt you to relax and get over yesterday."

I agreed to wait around for a while, which would give Rainy Day a little more time to recover from the night before. We talked about life in general, and Shawn told us more about his experiences overseas. Around noon Shawn started to yawn, and Aunt Patti and I tiptoed into the kitchen so he could nap on the couch.

"How about now?" I asked.

"You mean for going to Shady Glen?"

"Please?"

"I'm okay with it, I guess," Aunt Patti said. "But, ugh, April. Something tells me I don't have to be okay with stuff anymore in order for you to be perfectly fine."

"That means you're going to have to be okay with not

being okay," I said, getting two candy bars out of the junk drawer and holding them up. "Provisions for the next disaster," I said.

Aunt Patti clasped her hands to her heart and pretended to swoon with anxiety as I ran out the back door.

chapter

Rainy Day and I took it easy walking out of town. Everywhere I looked, the yards, roads, and sidewalks were a mess. Big orange service trucks were parked at every other intersection. Plattsburgh crawled with workers and volunteers cleaning up debris and digging out sewer drains. The sound of whining chain saws filled the air. Men from the electric company were perched up in the tall wooden poles along Route 50, repairing the long black wires that had come drooping down. I was careful to watch where we were going, and to give Rainy Day his head. Live wires were deadly.

Parked by the old Highway 47 bridge, a television van was broadcasting live news. On top of the van's roof, the remote transmitter cable was wound around a tall antenna. As Rainy Day and I crossed the bridge, I glanced down into the water below. Two trailer homes had wedged in odd angles into the bridge piers. On the far side of the bridge, a cameraman shouldered heavy-looking video equipment. He was filming the television reporter, who spoke gravely into a big black microphone while looking directly into the camera. Rainy Day and I kept going.

I followed the same route to Shady Glen that Aunt Patti and I had driven, going off the main road as soon as I could. Since the old Highway 47 was unpaved, this meant that we were in for a deep, sticky ride, but at least that was better than navigating through truck traffic.

Shady Glen came into view just as I was getting hot in the saddle. I let Rainy Day trot the rest of the way toward the main barn, and he stepped lively, as if he could sense how close we were to his friends. We were both happy to sweep around the long curve of the gravel driveway and see the three barns nestled in the valley below. Rainy Day snorted a greeting to the potbellied pigs and the tall emu grazing by the side of the road. Leigh came out of the barn and waved.

"Well, well! I sure am surprised to see you two," she said. "I hear things are mighty iffy down there in town." Leigh gave Rainy Day a long rub on his nose. "And how are you, my lucky man? You seem in fine form, don't you? How are things going, April?"

"Things are fine with me and Rainy Day," I replied. "But we've had a bizarre couple of weeks. Rainy Day's been amazing. You won't believe some of the things he's done. And this morning it occurred to me that he might like to visit some of his old friends."

"Well, I'm proud to say that everyone's doing great. We've had calls from all over the country asking about these horses, and people have been incredibly generous with their donations. We're set to care for them right here as long as we need to. None of them will ever have to work a day in their lives. Come on over and say hi to Calliope and Liberty. Get this guy unsaddled and let him go play."

I did as Leigh instructed and led Rainy Day over to the open paddock next door to the main barn. The two red roans watched us approach, swishing flies with their tails. Rainy Day trotted over to them merrily. I climbed up onto the bottom rail of the fence and watched.

"Calliope and Liberty made friends in the hospital," Leigh said. "They're pretty much inseparable now."

"How's the Thoroughbred, the stallion from Kentucky?" I asked.

"Honcho? Doing great. For some reason he's taken a shine to the miniature horse, Dexter. He and Dexter hang out in the riding ring together. They like rolling in that dust. I don't know if I told you this, but we rescued Dexter from a horrible, run-down petting zoo outside of Springfield. He'd been covered with mange and had worms. . . . It was horrible. Anyway, Honcho's got Dexter for a buddy and now he's gentle as a lamb."

Leigh's assistant called out and told Leigh she had a call.

"Gotta dash," Leigh said. "Feel free to stay as long as you'd like, April."

"Thanks," I said. Then I had a flash of an idea—maybe I ought to ask Leigh about working at Shady Glen for my summer job. That would be amazing. It was something to ask Aunt Patti about when I got home.

For a while I stood on the bottom rail of the corral fence and watched Rainy Day play with the two roans. He looked so happy, shaking his head and suddenly sprinting off. Eventually they all three went over to stand in the shade of a tall oak tree.

I hopped off the rail and walked back to the main barn. I poked around the stalls saying hi to all the horses and other animals. None of the horses had bandages on them anymore, but many had pink or gray bald patches where they had been injured. I looked into all their eyes and wondered just how deeply the wounds of their past had penetrated. I knew from Rainy Day that animals didn't only live in the present, that for them, like for us, the past existed in them. It was printed on their spirits somehow.

Some people say they love animals because of how simple they are, but ever since I had begun caring for Rainy Day, they did not seem simple to me. We do too much to them for them to remain simple, in my opinion. They figure their world out because they have to. They have no choice.

Kind of like kids.

The sun was blazing high in the sky when I saddled Rainy Day for our return ride. I was hungry for supper and figured Aunt Patti would need help taking care of Shawn, checking on her shop, and cleaning up around the house.

We trotted slowly up the hill out of the Shady Glen Valley and turned past the little cemetery and church on Belleview Road. As soon as we were on the old Highway 47, I clucked Rainy Day forward and he started at a quick trot. For some reason I felt lighter than air, as if a heavy weight had been lifted off my shoulders. Rainy Day seemed carefree, too. I knew he had enjoyed playing with his friends.

I clucked Rainy Day into a canter.

I could feel clumps of mud stick onto my boots and legs as he ran along the unpaved road. Hot air rushed into my face as we went. I felt completely solid in the saddle. I could hear and feel the three beats of the canter just the way Marty had described it the day he had drawn the hoof strikes of all the gaits on a piece of paper.

1-2-3

1-2-3

1-2-3

1-2-3

Before now, I had only cantered in the ring, which was smooth, but still, you were just going around in circles. Out on open road, I could really tell what the books meant when they explained that the canter is a much smoother gait than the trot. It felt like we were flowing. I couldn't help but wonder how much more fun it would be to go even faster. Of course, I remembered Marty's dire warnings about the gallop, how it was flirting with a horse's instinct to flee at top speed, even if that meant running straight into danger. But I also sensed I could trust Rainy Day not to do something stupid.

I loosened the reins, gave a small kick with my heels, and clucked him forward. "Come on, boy. Stretch your legs."

And that's how it happened—we were galloping. I squeezed tight with my legs, leaned forward, and both my hands fisted tightly around the reins in front of the saddle horn. I felt the three beats open up into four as Rainy Day stretched his head forward and let himself go. It was scary at first. Actually, it was scary the whole time, but scary in a good way. It was thrilling, not frightening. I couldn't see anything as the road and trees slid by in a blur. Rainy Day's hooves kicked clods of mud onto me, and I could feel little stones nipping at my legs. He kept going faster and faster but I held on, knowing that was all I would ever have to do—just hang on.

Just before the old road ended and we turned onto the new Highway 47, Rainy Day slowed down on his own. We were both panting. Returning to a walk, he adjusted the bit in his mouth and shook his head from side to side. Once he was more comfortable, we resumed a trot in the direction of East Hickory.

At home, I hitched him by the barn, gave him some water and fresh oats, and got out the supplies to give him his first thorough bath in ages: hose, shampoo, conditioner, grooming tools, towels, blanket, everything.

Aunt Patti doubled over in laughter when she came out into the yard and saw me hosing him down.

"What's so funny?"

"I guess you can't see yourself."

"Nope." I watched the water stream down Rainy Day's brown hair and puddle at his feet.

"You look like you've been dipped in caramel," she said.

"I'll shower when I'm done here."

"Sounds good. Maybe by then we'll have hot water again. Remember? No electricity, no hot water. Shawn just took a cold bath. How he managed that, I'll never know," she said, shaking her head.

"A little cold water won't kill me," I said, looking up at Aunt Patti.

There must have been something about the way I looked or sounded that made her hold her tongue.

With every day that passed, things calmed down around town. Shawn stayed put at our house. A new wheelchair had been delivered from the Veterans' Administration office in Eureka, and Aunt Patti said there was plenty of time to make new living arrangements when his mom came back from Little Rock in July.

"A lot depends on where I get accepted and what kind of financial aid packages are available," Shawn said. "And I wouldn't be starting school until January anyway."

One afternoon, a few days after the flash flood, I asked Shawn something that had been bothering me. We were sitting together on the front porch, watching Aunt Patti putter around in a far corner of the yard. She was weeding trumpet vines off the snowball bush. Rainy Day was grazing on long shoots of grass.

"You know the other night," I began, "when Rainy Day and I were approaching your doorway?"

"I don't think I remember that, no," he said, sarcastic as ever.

"Well, Rainy Day made this big half circle around your place. I thought he might actually be avoiding coming toward you. But then he paddled back and we made it. Is there some reason he did that, do you think?"

Shawn turned serious. "Actually, April, I had completely forgotten this but now that you mention it, yeah, the first round of flooding earlier on had brought down this massive dead elm right in front of my house. The whole crown of that tree was underwater the other day. If Rainy Day had swum through it, he would have gotten tangled up in the branches for sure."

"I figured it was something like that," I said. "Just checking."

The following Sunday Aunt Patti and I were supposed to drive into St. Louis to be with my grandma and the rest of the family, but after the flood we decided to stay in Plattsburgh. Aunt Patti and Miz Fran planned a big dinner feast and we all gathered at our house at four o'clock. Aunt Patti, Lowell, Miz Fran, Mr. Walt, Shawn, and I were hanging out on the back porch. Aunt Patti brought out a pitcher of what she called her summertime blend—iced tea mixed one to one with lemonade. Miz Fran had made a platter of deviled eggs, and there was a big bowl of potato chips and sour-cream-and-onion-soup-mix dip. Chase floated around, trying to get people to give him food.

"Ignore him, everyone," Aunt Patti said.

Eventually Chase lay down by Lowell, who had snuck him a cube of cheese.

Finally our garden plants had started to dry out. Butterflies and yellow jackets were dipping into the bulging pink hydrangea blossoms, and the small yellow lilies had opened up overnight. Aunt Patti's vegetable beds were filled with small green seedlings of lettuces and radishes. Delicate tendrils of young pea plants were beginning to climb up the string trellis. The fuzzy stems of tomato plants leaned into their wire cages for support. In the fenced corner by his barn, Rainy Day grazed peacefully.

Lowell had asked Shawn about being in the army. He thought it might be an option when he got done with high school.

"It just seems cool to be part of something that big," Lowell said. "I don't know. I don't think I'd like the fighting part, but all those drills, the exercises, the teamwork . . . in the commercials everyone just looks so...proud, or something. I've never been on any kind of team before."

I took a sip of my iced tea and waited to see how Shawn would respond.

"I know what you mean," Shawn said. "It all looked that way to me, too. Plus, I had my dad always talking about his army buddies and them doing this or that together. Hanging out, helping one another when they had to. But then you get into a situation—"

"Like Iraq?"

"Yeah, but it could be any war. You get into a situation and you're not just responsible for one another's lives, you're responsible for taking away other people's lives." Shawn paused. "I guess what I'm saying is, you don't have to be a soldier in an army to feel part of something big."

Nobody said anything. But Shawn didn't seem to be done. I hadn't heard him talk so much at one time ever before.

"What you and April did during these last few weeks, the way you guys saved..."

Shawn's voice went hoarse. I looked down. He continued. "You guys rose to service in exactly the way soldiers are expected to rise. And I wouldn't be here if you hadn't. You two are my kind of army."

"Hear, hear," Mr. Walt said, jumping in when he saw that Shawn was too emotional to go on. He came up behind Lowell and clamped an arm around his shoulders. "Cheers, everybody."

Listening to Shawn, it hit me again that he had gone off to join the army in good faith, and simply because that's what he thought he had to do. I looked at him sitting in his wheelchair and was reminded again of Black Beauty, and all the other horses who ever lived, who suffered just because they did what they were supposed to do. What if I had gotten Rainy Day all tangled in that tree and he had drowned? He would have died only because he had done what I was asking him to do.

Shawn, Rainy Day, and I—we were all survivors.

In the middle of supper, the telephone rang. Aunt Patti jumped up and ran into the living room to answer it. Through the open window we could all hear every word.

"Yes? Yes, this is she ... oh, hello, Joe ... yes, she's right here."

Aunt Patti pushed open the screen door and told me to come inside. I swallowed a mouthful of baked ham and took the phone.

"Hello?"

"April? Joe McCann."

"Oh, hi, Mr. McCann. How are you?"

"Well, I've had a bit of a spill."

"What do you mean?" I asked, concerned.

"The darndest thing. Earlier this morning I slipped and fell on that broken front step I've been meaning to fix. Had to call for an ambulance. Anyway, the hip is busted. Can't walk for some time and you know how things are around here. They sent me home until they can schedule an operation."

"I'm so sorry, Mr. McCann," I said.

"Oh, I'll be okay. But listen, I hate to trouble you, but do you think you might be able to get out here this evening for the chores? My son's on his way but can't get here till tomorrow. Hannah's in no shape to move much, and you know how things work around here."

"I'll check with Aunt Patti."

"I'll pay you, of course," Mr. McCann offered.

"I'm sure it'll be okay but... Mr. McCann?"

"Yes?"

I watched Lowell talk to Shawn. "Do you think there might be enough work for my friend, too?"

"I don't see why not," he said. "This place is a bottomless pit of work right now. But I'd like to meet him tomorrow to talk things over, if that's okay. "

I agreed to swing by alone in an hour and hung up.

"Hey, Lowell," I said. "Looks like we could get ourselves summer jobs at the McCann place," I said. "How are you with a hammer?"

"I guess I won't know until someone puts one in my hand."

At five-thirty I went over to Rainy Day, who had spent the whole afternoon turned out in the green grass. His eyes were shiny and clear as I hooked on the lead rope. We went into the barn to saddle up for the ride to Mr. McCann's. I lugged over the saddle pad and saddle and arranged them on his back. I paused before tightening the girth.

"Look at us," I said. "How did we end up like this, Rainy Day?" I rubbed his head on either side. "It can't be *all* because of an accident, can it?"

He rubbed the side of his nose against my arm and I continued getting him ready.

"You know what else," I said, chatting quietly in the cool barn. "This is the first Sunday afternoon I've spent in a long time not feeling sorry for myself."

I bounded into the saddle and urged Rainy Day toward the road out of town in the direction of the McCann place, where I would be spending so much of the coming summer. I imagined the days ahead—mucking stalls, feeding old Moses, gathering eggs, waiting for Hannah to deliver her foal—days I could not have imagined even a few weeks before. It was like when a train switches tracks: One lever flips, and the whole train with all its passengers goes to a totally different place.

"You gotta be on the lookout for those levers, Rainy Day," I said, clucking him into a faster pace. My horse opened up into a happy trot and I knew that this was going to be a perfect evening ride.

Glossary

Bay—a reddish brown color used to describe horses

bridle—the entire headpiece, including the bit, chinstrap, reins, and headstall

canter—one of a horse's four basic gaits, a three-beat gait

colt—a male horse under four years old that has not been castrated

croup—the rump, or back part, of the horse

currycomb—a plastic or rubber comb with several rows of short flexible bristles used for grooming

dock—the solid part of the animal's tail, not the hair

fetlock—the tufted, cushionlike projection on the back side of the leg above the horse's hoof

filly—a young female horse less than three or four years old

foal—a male or female horse less than one year old and still drinking their mother's milk

gallop—the fastest gait a horse can run

gelding—a male horse who cannot reproduce (unlike a stallion)

girth—a band or strap around the body of a horse that secures the saddle

halter—a harness of leather or rope that fits over a horse's head and is used for leading a horse

hock—the joint in the horse's hind legs similar to the human ankle

hoof pick—a metal or strong plastic tool with a pointed end for picking debris out of the underside of the hooves

mare—a female horse over four years old

Morgan—the oldest breed of horse originating in the United States, descended from a strong, fast, gentle, intelligient, and patient horse belonging to a Vermont schoolmaster named Justin Morgan in 1789

nicker—a sound a horse makes, presumably to communicate a greeting

paddock—an outdoor enclosure where horses are turned out for grazing

pastern—part of the leg between the hoof and the fetlock

pinto—a pattern of horse coloring characterized by two colors in particular patterns

poll—the topmost part of the head of the horse

rear—to rise up onto the hind legs

roan—a horse hair color characterized by a gray or white thickly interspersed with other colors such as bay, chestnut, brown, or gray

stallion—a male horse who can reproduce (unlike a gelding)

stifle—the joint in the horse's leg similar to a human knee

tack—all gear and equipment that can be worn by a horse, including the bridle, saddle, bit, and halter

Thoroughbred—a breed of horse used as a racehorse and for hunting and jumping

trot—a two-beat gait, with the legs moving together diagonally

walk—one of the four basic gaits, a four-beat movement where each leg moves independently and each hoof strikes the ground separately

withers—the slight ridge on the back of the horse

whinny—a low neighing sound